THE VOICE BEHIND THE WALL

A mass of sluggish hornets were clustered on the rug in front of a gap in the baseboard.

More in anger than in fright, Peter grabbed a wad of papers from the coffee table, rolled them into a makeshift tube and cleared the front of the opening of hornets. They moved willingly. He ran back to his desk, retrieved a length of cellophane tape, and wadded it as he went back to the baseboard.

Already another hornet, followed by yet another sluggish insect, was crawling through the space.

Peter thrust the wadded cellophane at the opening, pushing the two new intruders backward as the hole was plugged.

The sound of buzzing was very loud behind the wall.

And now, being this close to the wall, he noticed another sound. A rustling movement, a thin sound as if someone was scratching weakly against the other side of the wall.

And then a pained, tepid whisper.

"Peter..."

"What—"

He stood up, brushing a few slow-crawling hornets from the wall and put his ear flush against it.

It came again, the thinnest of rustling breaths heard behind a thick chorus of buzzing. *"Peter, help me."*

Other *Leisure* books by Al Sarrantonio:

Horror:
HALLOWS EVE
TOYBOX

Western:
WEST TEXAS

HORRORWEEN

AL SARRANTONIO

LEISURE BOOKS NEW YORK CITY

To
Joe R. Lansdale:
Buddy,
Heck of a writer

A LEISURE BOOK®

October 2006

Published by

Dorchester Publishing Co., Inc.
200 Madison Avenue
New York, NY 10016

ISBN 0-8439-5639-9

Visit us on the web at www.dorchesterpub.com.

HORRORWEEN

FOREWORD

The original name of the town was Orangefield, after a Scottish earl who was little remembered and therefore expendable. But the locals, by referendum in 1930, changed it to Pumpkinfield in order to make money.

"Hell, it *sounds* like Halloween!" was the general consensus. It was hoped that with a name like Pumpkinfield folks would come by and, if disappointed at the lack of pumpkins, would at least enjoy the foliage and spend dollars.

The second choice was Little Salem.

They didn't grow many pumpkins in the region in 1930, but in a bizarre case of the cart leading the horse, and then winning the race, it turned out that the soil was richly perfect and that pumpkins grew in profusion—up hillsides, in the fertile valleys, in straight tended rows, in backyard patches. By the late 1930s the place literally turned orange in late summer, and stayed that way until October 31st.

After that, with so many rotting (and smashed) pumpkins, the town smelled sickly sweet for a week.

Just before World War II, another referendum changed the name back to Orangefield.

It was sometime during this period that strange things began to happen in Orangefield—usually around the time of Halloween. There was the disappearance of the entire Cutler family in 1940, who left behind warm tea and a game of Monopoly in progress. Just after the War there was the murder of Amos Stone by his three children, wearing Halloween masks, aged seven, five and four, who then went on to murder one another, leaving a knife-induced bloodbath. In 1951 there was the brand-new Sullivan house, which went up in flames on its first All Hallows Eve, was rebuilt and burned down again the following Halloween. And then *again*. (The plot was left fallow after that.) These and other similar stories are covered in the first two volumes of this history.

There were, and continue to be, many tales of Samhain, the Celtic Lord of Death and master of Halloween, and many so-called "Sam Sightings." It has been said that Samhain somehow owns Orangefield, had claimed it before man of any kind—Native American or Englishman—had laid plow to the land. There occurred, during the writing of this history, the case of Hattie Ivers, and many others, who have claimed direct confrontation with Samhain.

And then there was perhaps the worst thing that ever happened in Orangefield, which concerned in part my own father, as well as the Pumpkin Boy, the children's book writer Peter Kerlan, the police detective Bill Grant and the three chosen by Samhain himself. . . .

—T. R. Reynolds, Jr.

Occult Practices in Orangefield and Chicawa County, New York, Volume Three

PART I

SOMETHING'S COMING

CHAPTER ONE

Too warm for October.

Staring out through the open door of his house, Peter Kerlan loosened the top two buttons of his flannel shirt, then finished the job, leaving the shirt open to reveal a gray athletic T-shirt underneath. Across the street the Meyer kids were rearranging their newly purchased pumpkins on their front stoop—first the bigger of the three on the top step, then the middle step, then the lower. They were jacketless, and the youngest was dressed in shorts. Their lawn was covered, as was Kerlan's, with brilliantly colored leaves: yellow, orange, a dry brown. The neighborhood trees were mostly shorn, showing the skeleton fingers of their branches; the sky was a sharp deep blue. Everything said Halloween was coming—except for the temperature.

Jeez, it's almost hot!

Behind him, out through the sliding screen door

that led to the backyard, Peter could hear Ginny moving around, making an attempt at early Sunday gardening.

Maybe it's cold after all.

He opened the front screen door, retrieved the morning newspaper he had come for and turned back into the house, unfolding the paper as he went.

In the kitchen, he sat down at the breakfast table and studied the front page.

The usual assortment of local mayhem—a robbery, vandalism at the junior high school, a teacher at that same school suspended for drug use.

In the back, Ginny cursed angrily; there was the sound of something being knocked against something else.

"Peter!" she called out.

He pretended not to hear her for a moment, then answered, "I'm eating breakfast!" and began to study the paper much more closely than it deserved.

On the second page, more local mayhem, along with the weather—sunny and unseasonably warm for at least the next three days—as well as a capsule listing of the rest of the news, which he scanned with near boredom.

Something caught his eye, and he gave an involuntary shiver as he turned to the page indicated next to the summary and found the headline:

HORNETS ATTACK PRESCHOOLERS

Another shiver caught him as he noted the picture embedded in the story—a man clothed in mosquito netting and a pith helmet holding up the remains of a huge papery nest; one side of the structure was caved in, and within he could make out the clumped remains of dead insects.

Again he gave an involuntary shiver, but went on to the story:

> *Oct. 7*
>
> *Orangefield, Special to the Herald—Scores of preschoolers were treated today for stings after a small group of the children inadvertently stirred up a hornets' nest that had been constructed in a hollow log. The nest, which contained hundreds of angry hornets, was disturbed when a kick ball rolled into it. When one of the children went to retrieve the ball, the insects, according to witnesses, "attacked and kept attacking."*
>
> *Twenty-eight children in all were treated for stings, and the Klingerman Preschool was closed for the rest of the day.*
>
> *The nest was removed by local beekeeper Floyd Willims, who said this kind of attack is very common. "The nests are mature this time of year and can hold up to five hundred drones, along with the queen. Actually, new drones are maturing all the time, and can do so until well into fall. With the warm weather this year, their season is extended, for another few weeks at least. The first real cold snap will kill them off."*
>
> *Willims continued, "Everyone thinks that yellow jackets are bees, but they're not. They're hornets, and can get pretty mean when the nest is threat-*

*ened. At the end of the season, next year's queens
will leave the nest and winter in a safe spot before
laying eggs and starting the whole process over
again with a new nest."*

As of last night, none of the hornet stings had
proved dangerous. Klingerman Preschool will re-
open tomorrow.

Peter finished the story, looked at the picture
again—the beekeeper holding the dead nest up with
a triumphant grin on his face—and gave a third involuntary shiver.

Ugh.

At that moment Ginny appeared at the back sliding door, staring in through the screen. He looked
up at her angry face.

"I can't get that damned shed door open!" she announced. "Can you help me *please?*"

"After I finish my breakfast."

Huffing a breath, she turned and stormed off.

"Aren't you going to eat with me?" he called after
her, hoping she wouldn't turn around.

She stopped and came back. "Not when you talk
to me with that tone in your voice."

"What tone?" he protested, already knowing that
today's version of *the fight* was coming.

She turned and gave him a stare, her huge dark eyes
as flat as stones. She was as beautiful as she had ever
been, with her close-cropped blonde hair and anything but boyish looks. "Are we going to start again?"

"Only if you want to," he said.

"I never want to. But I don't know how much more of this I can take."

"How much more of *what?*"

She stalked off, leaving the door open. After a moment, Peter threw down the paper and followed her, closing the sliding screen door behind him and dismounting the steps of the small deck. She was in front of the garden shed, a narrow, four-foot-wide, one-story structure attached to the house to the right of his basement office window.

"Well, I'm here," he said, not at all surprised that she momentarily ignored him.

Jeez, it is hot! he thought, looking up at a sun that looked summer-bright, and then surveying the backyard. The colored leaves fallen from the tall oaks that bordered the backyard looked incongruous, theatrical. There was an uncarved pumpkin on the deck of the house behind theirs; it looked out of place in the heat.

Peter turned to stare at Ginny's little garden, to the right of the shed, which displayed late annuals; they were a riot of summer color, which normally would have been gone by this time of year, killed by the first frost, which had yet to come.

"I've been weeding by hand," she explained, "but I'd like to get some of the tools out and get ready for next spring. I've been having trouble with the shed door again."

He stepped around her and pulled at the structure's wooden door, which gave an angry creak but didn't move.

"Heat's got the wood expanded. I'll have a look at it when I get a chance." He gave it a firmer pull, satisfied that it wouldn't move.

"Isn't there anything you can do about it *now*?"

"No." He knew he sounded nasty, but didn't care.

She reddened with anger, then brought herself under control. "Peter, I'm going to try again. We've been through this fifty times. You're punishing me, and there isn't any reason. I *know* it's been rocky between us lately. But I don't want it to be like that! Can't you just meet me halfway on this?"

"Halfway to hell?"

She was quiet for a moment. "I love you," she said, "but I just can't live like this."

"Like what?" he answered, angry and frustrated.

"No matter what I do, you find something wrong with it—all you do is criticize!"

"I . . . don't," he said, knowing as it came out that it wasn't true.

She took a tentative step forward, reached out a hand still covered in garden loam. She let the hand fall to her side.

"Look, Peter," she said slowly, eyes downward. "I know things haven't been going well for you with your writing. Believe me, I do. But you can't take it out on me. It's just not fair."

Male pride fought with truth. He took a deep breath, looking at her, as beautiful as the day he met her—he was driving her away and didn't know how to stop.

"I . . . know I've been difficult—" he began.

She laughed. "*Difficult?* You've been a monster. You've frozen me out of every corner of your life. We used to *talk*, Peter. We used to try to work things out together. You've gone through these periods before and we've always gotten through them *together*. Now . . ." She let the last word hang.

He was powerless to tell her how he felt, the incomprehensible frustration and impotence he felt. "It's like I'm dry inside. Hollow . . ."

"Peter," she said, and then she put a dirty, gloved hand on his arm. "Peter, talk to me."

He opened his mouth then, wanting it to be like it had been when they first met, when he had poured his heart out to her, telling her about the things he had inside that he wanted to get out, the great things he wanted to write about, his ambition, his longings—she had been the only woman he ever met who would listen to it, really *listen* to it. He had a sixth sense that if he did the wrong thing now it would mean the end, that he had driven her as far away as he dared, and that if he pushed her a half step further she would not return.

He said, "Why bother?"

Again, she reddened with anger, and secretly he was enjoying it.

"I'm going out for the day. We'll talk about this later."

"Whatever you say." He gave her a thin smile.

She turned away angrily, and after a moment he heard the screen door slide shut loudly, the front door slam and the muted roar of her car as she left.

Why did you do that? he asked himself.

And a moment later he answered: *Because I wanted to.*

CHAPTER TWO

The computer screen was still blank.

At the desk in his basement office, Kerlan sat staring at the clean white screen of the word processing program. It was like staring at a clean sheet of paper. *Maybe that's why they settled on that color, so that writer's block would be consistent in the computer age.*

He cringed at the words: *writer's block.*

After a moment he looked up over the top of the monitor at the casement window over his desk. Outside the sky was high and pallid blue and the window itself was open, letting the unnatural warmth in. It felt like late August.

While he watched, a hornet bumped up against the window screen, followed by another. After tapping at the unbroken screen in a few spots trying to find entry, they moved off with a thin angry buzz.

Not gonna get in here, boys.

Again the thrill of a shiver went up his spine as he remembered the story from the morning paper.

Too bad I can't turn that into a piece for Parade *magazine. . . .*

The phone rang.

He grabbed at it, as much in relief from the prospect of work as in annoyance.

"Pete, that you?" a falsely hearty voice said.

"Yeah, Don, it's me."

His agent Don Revell's voice became guarded. "I hesitate to bother you on a Sunday, but—"

"I'm not finished with it, Don."

A long slow breath on the other end of the line. "They need the story by Tuesday, Pete. Halloween's only three and a half weeks from today and they have to coordinate graphics with it and—"

"I know all that, Don," he said with annoyance. "It's just going slow is all."

"All that local research stuff you found—did it do you any good?"

"Fascinating stuff. But it hasn't helped me yet. I just can't seem to get a handle on this one."

"Jeez . . ." Revell started to sound frustrated, but held it in check. "Come on, Pete. You're one of the most popular children's horror authors on the planet. Your stories have sold in the millions in every language on Earth. You can do this stuff in your sleep. Bogey man, a nice little scare, kids save the day, end of story. Tuesday. Two days from now. Can you do it?"

"Sure I can do it. In their hands Tuesday."

"You sure, bud?" Revell sounded doubtful.

"No problem."

There was a hesitation. "You . . . sure you're all right, Pete?"

"Why do you ask?"

"You sound . . . weird. A little strange." A pause. "You been drinking?"

"Hell, no."

"Everything okay between you and Ginny?"

Maybe I should ask you that, you bastard.

He said with sarcasm, "Sure, Don. Just fine."

"Oh." After a long moment, Revell added, "Anything I can do?"

"Fifteen percent worth of advice?"

"No need to get nasty, Pete. I'm just trying to help."

Before Kerlan could stop himself it came out: "You've already helped plenty, Don."

The longest pause yet. "I told you, Pete, there was never anything between Ginny and I."

"You know how much I believe you, Don? Fifteen percent."

"Perhaps we shouldn't work together any longer, if that's the way you feel."

"You really want that, Don?"

"Actually, no, I don't. But if you can't get over this idea that Ginny and I had an affair, I think we'd better think about it."

Something far in the back of his mind, in the place that still was rational and mature, told him to stop.

He took a long breath. "Let's just forget it," he said.

There was a long breath on the other end of the line. "I'd like that, Pete. Get back to where things were."

Continuing in a reasonable tone, Kerlan said, "I'll have that piece in by Tuesday."

"Tuesday it is, bud. Maybe we can meet up early next week for a Halloween drink?"

"Sure, Don. Whatever you say."

"Talk to you soon."

"Right."

There was a click and the phone went dead.

He held it in his hand for a moment, staring at it. *Did she have an affair with him or not?* The truth was, he didn't know. He was smart enough to know that the root of his problem with Ginny was deeper than that—deeper in himself. She was perfectly correct when she told him that all of his problems were rooted in his own frustration with his writing. He knew that was true. But didn't everything else flow out of that? He'd always been a grouch—but had his moods grown so dark in the last months that he was actually driving her away from him?

Wasn't it reasonable to suppose that if he was driving her away, she would be driven into the arms of someone else? Someone like Don Revell, who was handsome, and younger than he was, and made plenty of money?

Did it matter that he had absolutely no evidence of an affair between the two of them, except for that fact that he realized he was such rotten company that she *had* to fall into someone else's arms?

That and the fact that he'd seen Revell put the moves on Ginny once?

God, Kerlan, you're an asshole.

18

He still loved Ginny, still loved her with all his heart, but had no idea how to tell her that.

The phone receiver still clutched in one hand, he lowered it slowly to its cradle and reached for the half-empty fifth of Scotch, which had been open since noon. He poured two fingers of the honey-colored liquid into the tumbler to the left of the keyboard.

I do think I'll have that drink with you now, Don, he thought, staring at the white sheet on the computer screen in front of him.

CHAPTER THREE

Four more fingers of Scotch and two hours later, he was no closer to filling the white blank space with words, but was at least enmeshed in the research in front of him.

Why the hell can't I get this down on paper?

It *was* fascinating stuff, the legends of Halloween and how they eventually became the relatively benign children's holiday of the present age. It was not always so. Halloween's roots were deep in pagan ritual, specifically the Celtic festival of Samhain, the Lord of Death. Samhain had the power to temporarily return the souls of the dead to their earthly homes. The Samhain festival had eventually turned into Halloween.

Why can't I turn this into a nice, not-too-scary children's story for the Sunday supplements?

He'd tried it a thousand ways—with pets, with witches, with scary monsters—but always it came out too frightening, too strong for children. Always it came out with Samhain as something not benign at all, but rather a hugely frightening entity to be feared more than life itself.

How the hell do you turn the Lord of Death into a warm, fuzzy character?

How the hell do you keep making a living, and straighten your life out, you dumb, useless bastard?

After another two fingers of Scotch, and another two hours, he gave up, went upstairs and fell asleep on the couch in the living room, dreaming of endless white pages filled with nothing.

CHAPTER FOUR

He heard Ginny come in, heard her hesitate as she beheld his prone body on the couch, heard her mutter, "Wonderful," and waited until she stalked off to the bedroom and slammed the door before trying to rouse himself. Blearily opening his eyes, he saw the orange sun setting through the living room window. It looked like a fat pumpkin.

Maybe there's something I can use there, he thought blearily. *A fat old pumpkin named Pete . . .*

He closed his eyes and drifted back to sleep.

A noise roused him. He knew it was much later, because it was dark through the window now. A dull white streetlight glared at him where the sun had been.

He stared at the grandfather clock in the adjacent dining room and saw that it was nearly eleven o'clock.

He heard noise off in the hallway leading to the front door. He hoisted himself into a sitting position on the couch. Head in his hands, he saw the empty Scotch bottle on its side on the floor between his legs.

"Wonderful indeed," he said, remembering Ginny's use of the word hours before, as the first poundings of an evening hangover began in his temples.

He stood, and discovered he was still mildly drunk.

And there, piled in the hallway leading to the front door, was much of what Ginny owned, neatly stacked and suitcased.

Holy shit.

He suddenly discovered he wanted another drink. He found his way to the liquor cabinet and was rooting around for an unopened bottle of Scotch when Ginny returned.

In a cold, even tone, she said, "Don't you think you've had enough to drink for one day?"

"Just one more, to clear my head," he said. "I get the feeling I'm going to need it."

She was beside him, her hand on his arm as he removed the discovered fifth of Dewars. To his surprise, her grip was gentle.

"Please don't," she said, and moved her hand down to take the Scotch from him.

Sudden resentment and anger boiled up in him. He pulled the bottle away, keeping it in his own hand. He turned away from her and twisted the cap off, looking unsteadily back into the living room for the glass tumbler he had used.

Ginny, amazingly, kept the gentle tone, but it had hardened slightly into urgency: "Please don't, Peter—"

"Just one!" he said, swiveling back to take a fresh tumbler from the top of the liquor cabinet where they stood, cut crystal sparkling like winking eyes.

He poured and drank.

"I really can't take this any longer," Ginny said quietly, and the continued mild tone of what she said made him focus on her.

"Take what? Me?"

"Yes."

He grunted a laugh. "So you're going to leave?"

"I think I have to."

"You gonna run to your lover? Fall into Don Revell's arms?" Even as he said it, even with his drunkenness, he knew it was a mistake.

Silence descended on the room like a cold hand. "I told you, Peter—"

He poured another drink, downed it. "You told me! You told me!" He waved the tumbler at her. "What if I don't believe you?"

With iron control she motioned toward the dining room table. "Sit down, Peter."

He moved the neck of the Scotch bottle to the tumbler, but her hands were firmer this time, yanking the bottle and glass out of his grip.

"Sit down."

He did so, fumbling at the chair until she pulled it out for him. He sat, and watched her sit on the opposite side of the table. Startled, he saw that there were tears in her eyes.

"I'm going to say this for the last time, Peter," she began, and suddenly he was focused on her as if he'd been struck suddenly sober. He knew by everything—her posture, her voice, the tears in her eyes—that this was the pivotal moment they had been moving toward for the past weeks.

"I'm listening," he said, the fight out of him before it had even begun.

She studied his face for a moment. "Good. Then please listen closely, because this is the best I can do to explain what's happened to us." She took a deep breath. "First of all, I never had an affair with Don Revell, and never would. He's your agent, and, quite frankly, I don't like him. He's smart, but he's ruthless, and the only reason he's with you is that you're making him money. We both know he would drop you in a second if you stopped producing."

Kerlan thought of his conversation that afternoon with Revell. "You're right about—" he began, but Ginny cut him off.

"Let me finish. I was merely being polite to him at that party in September. He tried to kiss me and I didn't let him. End of story."

"I saw—"

"You saw him *try*. I turned my cheek and let him peck me there. That's what you saw. After you turned away I told him as nicely as I could that if he ever tried to kiss me again I'd knee him in the balls."

Kerlan felt an odd urge to laugh—this sounded so much like the old Ginny, the one he had fallen in love with. But instead he just stared at her.

"You said that? You never told me—"

"You never let me tell you. For the last month you've been treating me like a leper. Ever since you started that Halloween magazine assignment Revell got you."

He found that his head had cleared to a miraculous extent. It was as if the importance of the moment had surged through him, canceling out the liquor.

"You know I've been having trouble with it."

Ginny laughed. "Having trouble? Like I said this morning, you've been nothing but a monster since you began researching it."

"The money's too good—"

"To hell with the money—and to hell with Don Revell! Just tell him you can't do it!"

"I've never had trouble with anything before—"

She leapt on his words as if she had been waiting for them. "Isn't that what this is all about, Pete? Isn't this all about you not being able to pull the trigger when you want to? It's always come easy, hasn't it? You've always been able to write when you wanted or needed to—and now for the first time you've got . . . writer's block!"

"Don't say that!" he nearly screeched. She had touched the nerve, and even she seemed to know she had gone too far.

"All right then," she said, backing off. "Let's just say you're having trouble with this one. Isn't that the root of all our problems lately?"

After a moment, when he found there was nothing else he could say, he said, "Yes."

She seemed to give a huge sigh of relief. In the

gentlest voice he had ever heard her use, she said, "Peter, do you think we can stop fighting?"

His eyes were drawn to the pile of her belongings waiting in the hallway. He found that the last thing in the world he wanted was for her to leave. To hell with his work—to hell with everything. He wanted her to stay.

"I . . . love you, Ginny. I'm . . . sorry for everything I've done."

Then suddenly she was around the table and holding him, and they both were crying.

"Oh, Peter, it's all right, everything's going to be all right."

"Yes, Ginny, I promise . . ."

"And you'll tell Revell you can't do that piece?"

He stiffened, and she pulled away from him.

"You'll tell him that?" she repeated.

The old anger tried to boil up in him—all the feelings of inadequacy, of helplessness, of everything that was mixed in with it, of him hitting middle age, getting older, afraid of losing his talent, afraid of losing *her*.

With a huge effort, he brought himself under control and said, "If it doesn't work in the next day or so, I'll toss it."

"You mean it?" Her huge beautiful eyes were searching his own, studying him, begging him.

Again he had to control himself, and knew she sensed it. "Yes."

She hugged him tighter. "I can't tell you how happy I am. I didn't want to leave. I was going to go to my sister's, and you know I can't stand her."

"Neither can I," Kerlan said dryly, and Ginny laughed.

"I love you more than anything in the world, Peter," she said, kissing him. "Don't ever doubt that."

She kissed him again, and Peter said, "I love you, too. More than you'll ever know."

She pulled away from him, smiling, and said, "I'll put everything away in the morning. It's Monday, and I want to get the rest of my gardening done early, before I go to work. I'll put my stuff away after I get home tomorrow night, all right?"

"All right," he answered, smiling back at her.

"You coming to bed?"

He almost said yes, sensing from the look in her eyes that she might want more than sleep, but instead he said, "I'm going to spend a little time in my office."

Her face darkened slightly. "You're not going to—"

"If it doesn't work immediately, I'm giving it up. Let's call this a last stand."

He could tell she was thinking of arguing, but instead she nodded. "All right, Peter. Give it one more try."

"I'll be up later."

She stopped, looked back at him. "I'll wait up for you, if I can keep my eyes open."

"See you later."

She went down the hall to the bedroom. Kerlan, grunting with the continuance of a well-deserved hangover, made his way downstairs.

CHAPTER FIVE

At three in the morning, he was finally ready to give up. The piece, no matter how he came at it, was just much too dark. The more he delved into the character of Samhain, the more frightening the Celtic Lord of Death became. There were hints of human sacrifice as tribute for good crops and prosperity. There were various dark tales of horrible deaths and evil perpetuated in his name. There was just no way to lighten him up. Peter tried making him into a character with a black cloak and pumpkin for a head, but when he read over what little he had written, the Lord of the Dead was just too scary for children. It just seemed that no matter what he tried to make the Samhain character do, he always ended up surrounded by death.

The *real* stuff.

And if little kids didn't like one thing, it was the real stuff.

He stared at a sketch he'd made of Samhain to help him, with the folds of his bright pumpkin head set back into the dark shadows of his cowl, a horrid sickle grin on his angular face, a spark of terrifying fire deep in the ebony eye sockets, stark white bone hands reaching from beneath the folds of the cloak. He shivered.

"Hell," he muttered to the picture, at the end of his rope, realizing that it just wasn't going to work, "*I'd* even pay tribute to you, Sam, if you'd help me finish this damn story."

Suddenly, as if a switch had been thrown, it came to him.

Sam. That was it! *Call him Sam.*

Just like in the local Orangefield myths and legends about Samhain, which the locals called "Sam sightings."

Almost before he knew it, he was tearing through the story, and, in what seemed like no time at all, it lay all but finished in front of him.

He came out of what felt like a trance, but what must actually have been, he realized, a mixture of waning work adrenaline, the remains of a Scotch hangover and just plain tiredness. Through the window above his desk, the sun had already circled the globe and come up over the back of the house. Brighter than it had been the evening before when it had hovered in the living room window, it now resembled a happy pumpkin.

By the clock, he saw that it was eight in the morning.

I worked five hours straight. Amazing.

Three tiny shadows passed by the window in front of the sun, hovering briefly before the screen, and he saw that they were yellow jackets. Briefly, he remembered the newspaper story from the day before. A shiver started, but was suppressed by tiredness.

He stretched, suddenly remembering Ginny.

I hope she just drifted off to sleep and didn't wait for me.

He rose, stretched as if his frame had been locked into a sitting position for a year, rubbed his eyes while yawning and left the office, tramping upstairs.

He thought of making coffee, but knew he would never stay awake while it brewed.

In the front hallway, he walked around Ginny's pile of belongings, noting with curiosity that the front door was open.

Upstairs, Ginny was not in the bedroom.

She was nowhere in the house.

On the pile of her belongings, perched like a bird, was a note:

Peter, I'm sorry, but I have to leave. . . .

CHAPTER SIX

"And there's a possibility the note may have been written the previous night, before your reconciliation?"

"Yes."

"Thing I don't get is, Mr. Kerlan, is why'd she leave without her things?"

Detective Bill Grant had been nice enough in the beginning, even solicitous; but now, standing with the man in the front hallway of the house, Peter sensed a change in the atmosphere, an aggressiveness that hadn't been present before. At first, all the questions had been about Ginny—where she might have gone, why she would have left; but now, Grant couldn't seem to take his eyes off the pile of belongings in the hallway. Peter could tell it stuck like a wad of gum to the roof of the man's mouth.

"I told you, Detective, we had a fight Sunday. A big one. I was sleeping on the couch when she came home, and when I woke up all of her stuff was in the hallway—"

"She packed while you were asleep?"

"Yes. And when I woke up we started the fight all over again. By the end of it we had squared things away, I thought. Ginny went up to bed and I went down to my office to work—"

"This was late, almost midnight?"

"Yes."

"And you worked through the entire night," Grant said, referring to his notes. "And when you went upstairs . . . ?" He looked up at Kerlan from his pad, and for the first time Peter sensed a faint belligerence from the man.

"When I went upstairs she was gone."

The detective snapped his fingers. "Just like that?"

"Yes."

"Left her belongings, her car, just took off after you had *supposedly* settled everything?" He gave a twist in emphasis to the word "supposedly," making it sound almost sinister.

"That's exactly right."

"And you called us after you spent yesterday looking everywhere she might have gone, including her sister, an . . ."—he consulted his notes—". . . uncle in Chicago, her best friend from college and even your own mother." He glanced sideways from his notebook at Kerlan. "*Your* mother?"

"My mother and Ginny are very close. I could see her going there, yes. Ginny's own parents are dead."

Grant nodded briefly, went back to his notes. "You

called all the local motels and hotels . . . that about the whole story?"

"Yes."

Grant straightened, turning his notebook to a new page. "Well, maybe not exactly, Mr. Kerlan. I'd like to fill in a few blanks, if you don't mind."

"Anything you want."

"All right, then. Let's see . . ." Grant was running his eyes down a notebook page, flipped back to the previous page and did the same. He had the sallow, heavy-lidded look of a heavy drinker. But his eyes, which were bright blue in a rough, stubbled face, making them startling, pinned Peter suddenly.

"Let's start with you being asleep on the couch on Sunday. You were taking a *nap*?" Again the emphasis on a word, this time "nap," which made Grant sound incredulous.

"I'd had a few drinks, and was sleeping that off."

"Ah." This seemed to satisfy Grant, and he went on searching his notes. Kerlan had the feeling that the detective already had a list of laser-sharp questions in a neat list in his head, and was only scanning the notebook for effect.

"You had *two* fights with your wife that day?"

"One at breakfast time and then another that night."

"You fought a lot?"

"Recently, yes."

"Marital . . . trouble?" Grant let his hand wander in the air, waving his pen in a little circle to make the question more than it was.

37

"I've been having trouble with my work. It carried over."

"Any other obvious difficulties? Money? Sex life? You having an affair, maybe?"

Kerlan blinked, surprised at the question. "No. Nothing like that."

"Nothing like that." Grant nodded to himself, making a note on his current page. "You drink a lot, Mr. Kerlan?"

Again, he was taken aback. "No. Occasionally I have a few."

"Have a few. . . . You ever hit your wife? Slap her around?"

Now Peter became angry. "No."

Grant nodded, made a note. "You can't think of anywhere else she might have gone, anyone else she might have gone to see?"

"No."

The detective eyed the pile of goods stacked in the hallway for perhaps the twentieth time. "Any idea why she left her stuff behind, Mr. Kerlan?"

"That's the part I don't get."

"Me too. If you were running away, would you leave all your things behind after spending the time and trouble to stack it all up in the hallways by the front door?"

"No, I wouldn't."

Suddenly the detective straightened again, turning it into a stretch. He flipped the notebook closed and pocketed his pen in the side pocket of his jacket. His tie was loosened, Peter noticed.

Without warning, Grant smiled, making Peter blink.

"Thanks, Mr. Kerlan. I've got everything I need for now. We'll check over everything you've done already, and widen the motel and hotel search a little into the next county. It's kind of early yet to be too worried. I'll be in touch." He suddenly winked, and held out his hand. "If she shows up give me a call, will you?"

Peter went to shake the hand but then saw that there was a business card in it, which he took automatically.

"I will, Detective."

"Do that." Grant turned on his heels and was out the front door and into his sedan almost before Peter could answer. Peter saw him light a cigarette as he climbed into the car.

He watched the detective pull out of the driveway over a mat of unraked leaves. In the last two days the trees had almost denuded themselves completely, leaving a riot of reds and yellows on his lawn. Peter idly noticed that the Meyers had cleared and bagged their own front yard, the neatly clipped grass of which showed yellow-green. Their three pumpkins had settled into a neat row—smallest at the top, fattest of the three at the bottom. In their picture window were Halloween cutouts: a jointed white skeleton with a toothy grin, a black-clad witch riding a broomstick angled up toward a sickle reddish moon.

Halloween was only three weeks away.

And it was still too damned hot.

He turned away from the front door, confronted by the mute pile of Ginny's belongings.

For a moment, tears welled up in his eyes.

Ginny, where are you? I thought we had fixed it? I thought we were okay?

The boxes, the suitcases, the bags of clothing, remained mute.

CHAPTER SEVEN

He first felt not a sting, but the vague, insistent, faint, tiny itch of an insect on his leg.

He swiveled in his armchair, bending his left leg and at the same time brushing at the itch; something small, dark and solid dropped from his leg and melded with the carpet beside his desk. It wriggled there for a moment, righting itself in a tiny lifting of small wings, and he bent to examine it, suppressing a sudden shudder.

It was a hornet, not much past pupae stage, its tiger stripes muted into almost orange and black.

He remembered the story in the newspaper, the children stung by a legion of hornets from a nest they had disturbed. . . .

"How in hell?" he said, lifting his plush slipper almost without thinking to grind the insect into the carpet before it could advance or possibly take flight.

Suppressing another shudder, he drew his foot

away, dragging it across the carpet to rid the slipper's bottom of the creature's remains. A diminishing line of bug guts, looking dry and powdery and papery, trailed the low-cut gray rug till they came to a point and disappeared.

Have to clean that later, he thought, turning back to his work.

The basement office's single screened window was open above his desk, and for a moment he idly heard a buzz and looked up.

There, outside, was a fat bumblebee, just bumping the screen before lumbering airily off.

Before turning back to his work he let his eyes roam over the screen, looking for torn corners or holes; there were none.

Didn't get in that way.

He turned back to his work, which was still going well; after sending the Halloween story to *Parade* magazine on Monday he'd discovered he had more to say on the subject of Samhain—or, as he called his own cute little version, Sam.

Almost immediately the phone rang, and he clutched his pencil, almost throwing it down angrily before dropping it on the desk and, with a sigh, picking up the receiver.

"Yes?"

It was Revell on the other end of the line, asking after him.

"I'd be doing a lot better," Peter said, trying to keep the testiness out of his voice, "if I didn't have people like you bothering me."

Revell said with false concern, "I'm just worried about you, Pete."

Are you?

"Thanks for the concern."

"You heard anything more from the police?"

"No. They don't have anything new." *Unless Ginny's with you after all, you bastard.*

"Well, let me know if you need anything," Revell said. "I—"

Peter cut him off. "I really have to get back to work."

"Nothing wrong with that. Take your mind off what you're going through. Actually, that's the reason I called—"

Of course it is, you bastard. He recalled what Ginny had said: "He would drop you in a second if you stopped producing. . . ."

"I've got to go. I'll call you soon."

Like hell I will.

He slammed the phone down, stared at the wall next to his desk.

Something was crawling up it, above the wooden filing cabinet that held his printer—muted orange and black stripes . . .

"What the fu—"

He reached out a palm, hit it flat; the hornet, still whole, tumbled from the wall behind the filing cabinet and was lost from view.

He was on his feet, pushing his swivel chair back and pressing his head against the wall to try to locate the insect behind the cabinet; unable to, he stalked from the office in anger and went to his messy workbench at the other end of the basement, pushing objects aside—a power screwdriver, a coffee tin of miscellaneous nails—until he located a flashlight. He turned back toward the office, flipping the flashlight switch, which produced a click but no lightbeam.

"Shit!"

He reversed stride, rummaged through the wreckage on top of the workbench, then pulled drawers open until he found an opened four pack of D cells; he unscrewed the flashlight's top, turned it over impatiently, dropping one of the two batteries within to his waiting palm and the other to the floor, where it rolled beneath the bench.

"Shit! *Shit!*" He kicked the bench once, then pulled back his slipper to kick it again before breathing deeply and turning his attention to the new batteries, which he shoved viciously into the flashlight's tubular body before screwing the head back on and flipping it on once more.

Light shone this time, then blinked out until he smacked the tool against his palm, hard.

The beam stayed on.

He strode back to the office and played the beam on the wall above the filing cabinet. Getting closer, he was about to shine it behind the cabinet when he saw an immature hornet crawling over the printer's paper tray, and another on the wall beside it.

He cursed, put the flashlight down on the desk, looked for something to hit the insects with and found a recent trade journal, which he rolled up, smacking the two hornets with it.

One dropped away to the rug; the other lay squashed against the printer's paper roll.

Wary now, he looked in increments behind the printer, saw another insect making its way up the wall behind, and what looked like two others below it, showing movement.

Shivering, he drew back, moved away from the desk and toward the office's door, his eyes glancing at the rug, the walls, the ceiling.

He closed the door behind him, dropped the rolled up magazine and climbed the steps to the house's first floor two at a time.

He made his way to the front door, pushing his way past piles of Ginny's clothes, Ginny's books, her CDs.

He yanked open the front door, pushed open the screen, descended the porch's four steps and walked quickly to the western rear corner of the house, which fronted his basement office and the bedroom above it.

The cable television and phone line entry, as well as the house's gas main, were clustered near the side corner. He examined them, seeing no entry for an insect where the wires and gas line led into the house's siding; everything was sealed and caulked.

He moved closer; a hornet flew past him, then another, and he spotted the entry, below the siding level. He watched a moment, saw a hornet fly to a spot near the corner of the house where foundation met siding, land and crawl underneath the siding.

Edging closer, he crouched nearly to the ground, turning his head to examine beneath the siding.

There was a gap there in the wooden sill plate on which the house rested above the concrete foundation; it looked like the two boards that met at the corner had either not been properly butted, or that the butting board had shrunk, leaving an opening into an area between the house's first floor and basement.

"Jesus," he said, as a hornet crawled out from the space, flying past him with a rush as another crawled into the opening.

They had obviously built a nest back there.

"*Damn.*"

Filled with fury and resolve, he got to his feet, returned to the house and kicked his slippers off in the living room, looking for his deck shoes; they were nowhere to be seen and he searched down the hallway, almost reaching the back bedroom before finding the shoes nestled one against the other just outside the bedroom door.

He slipped them on, checked the pockets of his shorts for his car keys and then moved back outside, slamming the house door behind him.

I'll take care of you, you bastards.

He got into his Honda, nearly leaving rubber as he backed out of the driveway, and was back in twenty minutes with two cans of hornet and wasp killer. Barely reading the instructions, he pulled the safety tab from the top of one can, shoved the thin, hard plastic straw that came with it into the can's top nozzle and shook the can as he marched back to the outside corner of the house.

Want to eat this? Enjoy it!

He stopped before the spot, watched a hornet alight and then crawl into the hidden opening, watched another crawl out and fly off. He crouched, thrusting the can's nozzle forward and awkwardly trying to fit it under and into the opening.

The hard plastic straw missed, sliding away as a hornet, angered, crawled out, followed by another.

Flinching, he pressed the nozzle, watching the acrid spray cover the two insects; they froze and dropped to the ground.

And now the rest of you bastards.

Still spraying, he crouched lower, his eye level below that of the foundation, and found the opening.

He angled the nozzle's straw in and tightened his grip on the can's trigger.

A single hornet fought its way out, then dropped immediately to the ground. Another, coming from the outside, circled the opening, caught a whiff of escaping spray and also dropped.

He emptied the can, then pushed himself back as three returning hornets began to circle the hole widely; one of the insects ventured into the hole, immediately retreated and then dropped to the ground. There was a long stain of spilled pesticide spray down the foundation under the hole, which began to dry as he watched.

A cloud of hornets circled the sprayed opening, darting toward it, landing tentatively on the lowest level of siding over the opening, then took off again.

He shook the can, let a final spray cover them; all but one dropped to the ground as the remaining one flew off.

That'll take care of you.

Breathing deeply, the adrenalin rush that had sustained him for the past hour receding, he went into the house, scooping up the second can of insect spray where he had deposited it on the front stoop, in time to hear the telephone begin to ring.

It was Don Revell again.

"Pete, I'm sorry to bother you again, but you didn't let me finish before. *Parade* was so wild about that Halloween piece you did that I showed it to Doubleday and they flipped. They'd like you to do more, and turn it into a book. We're talking high five figures, maybe low six for this one—"

"I'll think about it."

"Jeez, what's to think about? Just say 'yes' and I'll take care of the rest. They're talking about publishing next Halloween, cash register dump display, a real push. These characters of yours could become perennials—you could turn one out every Halloween, have the kids waiting in line—"

"I said I'd *think about it*—"

"I know you're worried about Ginny, bud, but this one could set you up with a guaranteed every year for the next five years at least. Can I at least negotiate a three book deal?"

He said nothing, and Revell went on: "The characters are great, Pete! A real Halloween character!

Named Sam no less! And I *love* Holly Ween! I've got feelers out already to television, and I think we can expect a *big* bite on that—half hour like *It's the Great Pumpkin, Charlie Brown*. We're talking ancillary—lunch boxes, T-shirts, the whole nine—"

"Do whatever the hell you want!" Kerlan shouted, and slammed down the phone.

He gripped the receiver tightly as he suddenly began to cry.

If she wasn't with Revell, she was with someone else.

And he'd driven her away.

She's gone and I know it. Gone for good.

He let the second can of bug spray slip to the floor as he covered his face with his hands and wept, and kept weeping.

CHAPTER EIGHT

After trying to watch television, and trying to eat, he went to bed early and as a consequence rose early the next morning.

With a tepid cup of instant coffee in his hand, he made his way down to the basement office.

Even before reaching it, the faint, acrid smell of bug spray tickled his nostrils.

"Christ," he said, wincing as he walked into the room; it was even worse than the faint, musty odor the basement room sometimes held in the summer months, when the foundation walls behind the sheet rock-covered studs picked up humidity from the ground. The smell had been particularly noticeable this year.

He stood up on his swivel chair, cursing sharply as it started to turn sideways under his weight, then leaned out over his desk to open the room's single casement window.

"Shit," he said, recoiling; in the casement box were the bodies of five small hornets, all but one seemingly dead; the live one moved feebly, its small wings opening once, then again. Behind the casement, somewhere behind the room's wall, he heard a faint buzzing sound.

He climbed down from the chair, nearly ran to the workbench area and returned with the basement's wet-vac.

He plugged the vacuum into the wall socket between his desk and the printer stand, turned it on and angled the hose nozzle up into the casement, sucking up all of the hornets.

His eye caught movement by the printer, and he saw another small insect crawling up the wall over the machine.

I thought I wiped you bastards out yesterday!

He covered the hornet with the sucking nozzle, then looked wildly around the walls, then at the floor.

"Shit!"

There was a cluster of dead bodies fanned out in the corner just to the left of the printer stand, where a heat register ran across the wall at floor level; two live hornets were just crawling out of the bottom of the register itself.

"Shit! *Shit!*" he said, fighting an uncontrollable chill, thrusting the vacuum head around the area and plugging it into the corner under the register as far as it would go.

He heard the tap of insect bodies rushing up the

vacuum's soft plastic accordion hose and into the wet-vac's drum.

Another crawled out onto the rug from behind the printer stand, and he speared it, then put the nozzle back into the corner. He kept it there, feeling another tiny body sucked up into the machine, and then another.

He gave up all thoughts of work and fled the office; at the doorway he saw a feebly moving hornet on the rug by the sill, and mashed it with his foot, closing the door behind him.

CHAPTER NINE

"Sounds weird enough, Mr. Kerlan, but they all sound weird to me. One time—"

"Can you come today?" Peter said into the phone, cutting the beekeeper off before he went into yet another anecdote. "This infestation is in the place I work, and I need it taken care of."

"Sure," the other said, slowly. "I suppose I can be there this afternoon. We'll take care of you."

"I hope so," Kerlan said, slamming down the phone.

He stole a glance into his office, opening the door a crack. By now all sorts of nightmares preyed on his mind: the room filled with flying insects; a swarm waiting for him, covering him as he opened the door . . .

All inside seemed quiet; the casement window threw a rectangular shaft of light against the far wall's built-in bookcase. He opened the door wider, listening for buzzing.

Maybe I wiped them out after all.

His relief was short-lived; as he stepped toward his desk his foot covered three squirming hornet bodies, and he saw a few more scattered here and there, some unmoving, others moving as if drugged; there were also three or four on the walls, and more, perhaps a dozen, covering the casement's window itself, silhouetted dots against the light.

He reached for the wet-vac, recoiling as a hornet brushed his hand as it fell from the hose; others were crawling over the instrument's drum, one hiding coyly by one of the rolling wheels.

Once again he fled, closing the door behind him.

"What you've got here is a classic case of wall infestation," the beekeeper, whose name was Floyd Willims, said. He *looked* like a beekeeper, was tall and thin-haired and preoccupied when he stepped from his dirty white van; and now even more so, dressed almost comically in a pith helmet, the brim of which was ringed with mosquito netting. From the back of his van he pulled a thick pair of rubber gloves from a soiled box. He held up the gloves for inspection. "Triple thickness," he said, almost proudly. "Stingers can't get through." After retrieving a powder-filled canister and what appeared to be a pump hose from the van, he turned back to Kerlan and said, "Proceed!"

Kerlan had already showed him the corner of the house where the hornets had gained access; they returned to that spot now and the beekeeper knelt, put the thin end of the hose that led into the canister in the opening and began to puff powder into it.

"This'll kill 'em dead," he said. "Whichever ones return will carry the powder into the nest and spread it to the others."

As if on cue, as the beekeeper removed the hose from the opening a hornet alighted and crawled into it.

"Now let's have a look at the nest," the beekeeper said, heading for the house with Kerlan.

They had already studied the office on the beekeeper's arrival, and the beekeeper had helped Kerlan move furniture so that the upper corner of the wall, behind which the beekeeper said they would find the nest, was exposed; luckily, there would be access through a nearby panel, behind which the house's electrical box was located. To either side of the box was packed insulation, which the beekeeper began to remove.

The smell of insect spray became stronger in the room.

The beekeeper lay the strips of insulation on the floor. Kerlan was repulsed to see hornets crawling feebly over the pink spun glass fibers of its back.

The beekeeper held up a strip and examined the five hornets on it carefully.

"You zapped them pretty good with that off the shelf stuff you sprayed into the nest yesterday," he said. "If you'd gotten them at dusk, when they were all in the nest, you might have killed them all. What we're looking at are the dregs, I think."

"How did they get in here to begin with? How many openings does the nest have?"

Willims had shown him a picture of a typical paper hornet's nest, a nearly round structure with a single opening, usually at the bottom.

"They either made another exit, or left an opening near the top," he said. "This isn't quite a typical nest. They were drawn to the light in your office." He pointed to the baseboard, the corner of the floor where the heat register butted the wall. "There's an opening down there, I'm sure. Doesn't take much, just a quarter inch." He squinted through his mosquito netting at the molding along the rug where the printer stand had been before they moved it. "There may be others. Like I said, a quarter inch is all they need."

An involuntary chill washed over Kerlan as a hornet crawled onto the beekeeper's glove and onto his shirt sleeve. The beekeeper regarded it for a moment and then flicked it to the floor. "Like I said, you must have hit them good. If they were healthy they'd be all over us because of the light." He turned to Kerlan as if having a sudden thought. "Sure you don't want to leave?"

"I'll stay, if you think it's safe."

The beekeeper laughed. "Safe enough. If they pour out of the walls when I remove the rest of this insulation, I'll yell and you can run."

Kerlan's eyes enlarged in alarm, but the beekeeper added, "Not likely to happen."

At that moment the beekeeper pulled the last strip of insulation out with a grunt.

Nothing happened; the beekeeper angled his head, aiming a flashlight up into the exposed cavity, and called back, "Yeah, you hit 'em pretty good."

Kerlan leaned over, trying to see; Willims pulled back a strip of insulation and a fist-shaped clutch of dead hornets fell from the space between the open cavity and the beekeeper's body.

The beekeeper angled his arm up into the cavity. "I'll . . . get it out if I can."

He pulled a huge chunk of dark papery gray material out of the cavity, then let it drop to the floor.

"Nest," he said in explanation. It was followed by a bigger chunk, mottled and round on the inside; within its crushed interior were dead hornets and a few feeble live ones.

"Ugh," Kerlan said.

"Pretty big nest," the beekeeper said, continuing to pull sections of the structure out. Mixed with the leavings were the familiar honeycombed sections that Kerlan knew contained the pupae. Most but not all were empty.

"About the size of a soccer ball. They built it right up in the corner beneath the floor above. As they built the nest it forced the insulation back. Amazing critters," said Willims.

He continued his work, and Kerlan shivered.

* * *

An hour later the office was more or less back to normal, and Kerlan was writing the beekeeper a check.

"You'll want to caulk that hole they used in a couple of weeks," Willims said. "That powder I sprayed around it will take care of any stragglers."

"Why not plug it now?"

"Well, you could, but there could still be a few females outside the nest; they'd just start another one."

Kerlan had forgotten that each nest held a queen. "Didn't we kill off this nest's queen?"

"You can be pretty much certain of that. But even so, any female can become a queen. They'll just start another nest." He grinned. "Hornet season's not quite over, you know. I'll be getting calls like yours 'til mid-November, if the heat holds out."

"Christ."

The beekeeper folded the check and turned toward his dirty white van. Kerlan had a sudden thought.

"You're sure my nest is dead?"

The beekeeper shrugged. "Pretty sure. You may see a few strays wander out of your baseboard gaps looking for light, but believe me, that nest is dead. Only other problem you could have is if two females got in there originally and the second one started another nest somewhere else inside the wall, farther down." Seeing Kerlan's eyes widen he laughed. "Not likely that happened, though. Plug the gaps in the baseboard if you can; you can use a wad of scrunched up cellophane tape. Call me if you have any more problems."

Kerlan nodded as the van drove off.

A single yellow jacket brushed by his face as he entered the house.

CHAPTER TEN

The next morning he entered his office to work. The evening before, he had moved along the edge of the baseboard where he could get at it, pushing cellophane tape into anything that looked like an opening. By the baseboard he had found a huge hole surrounding the heat pipe which led into the register; around it were tens of dead yellow jackets and a very live spider as big as a thumbnail feeding on them. There was a sour smell emanating from the vent: a mixture of fading bug spray and the strong damp smell from the cavity behind. After recoiling, he cleaned the area out with the wet-vac and then plugged it with insulating material. The smell receded.

He vacuumed the rug thoroughly, sucking up dead hornet bodies, and then replaced his furniture and turned on his computer.

There came a tapping at the casement window above him and he started, looking up; it was just a fat bumblebee, probably the same from the other day, which ambled sluggishly off.

He let out a deep breath and turned to the screen.

He typed out the words *Sam Hain and the Halloween that Almost Wasn't* and quickly became lost in the characters as words poured out of him in a torrent. Nothing like this had happened to him in the last twenty years. Page after page scrolled down the screen, and he knew they were all good. He finished one story and the ideas for two others came into his head unbidden. He typed so fast his fingers began to ache—something he hadn't felt since the days of electric typewriters, when the constant kickback of the keys would rattle his knuckles and literally make his fingers sore. It was a marvelous feeling. And still he wrote on, completing outlines for two more stories before finally letting himself fall back into his swivel chair, breathing hard. It was as if he had run a marathon, and he couldn't believe the mass of material now stored on his hard disk.

Without thinking, he sent it all as an attached file to Don Revell, with a curt note: "Like I said, do whatever the hell you want."

He knew that would keep the bastard busy for a while, and off his back.

Even now, he felt another itch at the back of his brain, which would turn into more work tomorrow. He knew it. It had been so long since this had happened to him, this creative torrent, that he'd forgotten what it was like.

Oh, Ginny, if only you were here now! The problem's gone! I can write again!

It was the only sour note in what had been a marvelous day. He looked up at his casement window and saw that night had fallen, and that a waxing moon was rising. It looked huge and orange-tinged, and even that gave him a new idea for a story: *Sam and Holly and the Halloween Moon.*

Quickly he wrote it down in outline, and when he looked up again the moon was high and the clock said it was midnight.

He stumbled upstairs, past Ginny's things, and walked down the hall to bed, where he dreamed of black and orange things, and a cute character named Sam Hain, a squat fellow that looked like a comical skeleton with a wide happy grin and a spring in his step, who danced through a children's Halloween world with his blonde-curled friend Holly. It was a world of orange and yellow and red, of perpetually falling leaves that danced and dervished, and trick-or-treat bags that were always open and bottomless, and jack-o'lanterns that never sputtered or grew burned black inside or soft rotten, and winds that were blustery and just cold, and clouds that made the fat full moon wink, and a night that was always All Hallows Eve, with hoots in the air, and scary costumes that weren't really scary at all . . .

And in the dream Sam Hain changed, even as the night changed, as he grew from a fat happy children's character into a monstrous terrifying thing, black and tall and cold as ice, his bone hands white and hard as smooth stones, his eyes deeper than black empty wells, his grin not happy but ravenous, his breath ancient and colder than space and sour with death as he bent to whisper into Kerlan's ear something soft and horrible, something that made him scream even as it filled him with joy . . .

Two days, it said. *You'll see her in two days.*

He awoke, covered in sweat, with the moon higher than his window and the night suddenly chilly, and for a moment he thought he saw something that looked like Ginny lying on the bed next to him, something that turned to writhing tiny balls of dust and then vanished.

He sat up in bed breathing heavily, drenched in cold sweat, eyes wide with fear, and then he lay down again, and the room grew warm, and he slept again, dreamless.

CHAPTER ELEVEN

The day next he sat in front of his screen again obliviously typing until a sound, a tiny insistent buzzing, made him look up.

He already had outlines for two more Sam Hain stories and was in the middle of a third. Groggily, he glanced up at his window and saw a hornet buzz by outside the screen.

He went back to work, but the tiny insistent buzzing remained. It was like an itch at the back of his mind.

If anything, the weather had grown even hotter. The radio, which he had listened to briefly while making coffee, mentioned the day as a record-breaker of eighty-two degrees for this date, October 12th. The leaves on the front lawn were wilting, turning dry and crackly like they normally did in deep winter. The Meyer kids, he barely noticed, were now all in shorts and short sleeve shirts.

As he worked, the faint buzz remained, but he tuned it out and kept tapping at the keys.

Sometime in early afternoon, after ignoring two phone calls, he hit a lull and reached blindly for the phone when it rang again.

"Yes?" he said curtly.

There was a slight pause, and then a voice said: "Mr. Kerlan? This is Detective Grant."

For a moment that meant nothing to him, but then he focused on the name.

"Are you there, Mr. Kerlan?" the detective asked.

"Yes, I'm here."

"I was wondering if you've heard from your wife."

He remembered the dream from the night before. "Have *you* heard from her?" he said with hope.

Again a pause. "No, I haven't. Frankly, I don't see why I would. I'm just checking in to see if by any chance she made contact with you, or anyone else you know."

"I haven't heard from her."

"That's too bad." Another pause, which Kerlan waited patiently through.

"Mr. Kerlan, do you mind if I ask you a few more questions?"

Peter's attention now was on everything Grant said. His hands left the keyboard reluctantly. "Sure, go ahead."

"Thank you. I was . . . wondering if perhaps your wife had gone to . . . someone other than a family member?"

"Like who?"

"Someone . . . perhaps she was . . ." Grant laughed

with slight embarrassment. "I don't know quite how to say this, except to just say it."

Peter waited.

"Mr. Kerlan, was your wife having an affair?"

He instantly thought of Revell.

"Who told you that?"

"Well . . . I shouldn't say this, but one of her relatives told me that there had been some . . . friction between your wife and yourself lately over the question of her, perhaps, seeing someone else. . . ."

A kind of relief flooded through him; he'd thought perhaps the detective had dug up facts when, in fact, he had obviously been talking to Ginny's big-mouthed sister, who would have known about their problems.

"Did Ginny's sister Anna tell you that?"

Grant said, "Well . . ."

"If she did, there's nothing to it. I had a fit of jealousy, but there was nothing behind it."

"That's what your agent said when I talked to him, but you never know with these things. People try to . . . keep things quiet sometimes. . . ."

"Revell."

"Yes, Don Revell. So as far as you know your wife wasn't having an affair with Mr. Revell?"

"Absolutely not."

"But you *did* think she was, for a time."

"For a brief time, yes. I was wrong."

"Jealousy, you said . . . ," Grant replied, and Peter could picture the man consulting his cursed notepad, flipping pages.

"Is there anything else, Detective? I'm busy—"

"Just a few more questions. Unless you'd like me to drop by later. . . ."

Peter sighed. "That's all right. I'll answer whatever you want now."

"Thank you for taking the time, Mr. Kerlan. Now . . ."

Peter could *hear* the rustling of notebook pages. He waited.

Grant finally said, "Ah. What I wanted to know was, is it possible, I mean, could it be possible, that your wife is not missing, but has been murdered?"

Peter's vision went black for a moment. "What?"

"What I mean is," Grant said, in the same casual tone, "do you think it's possible?"

"Murdered? By whom?"

"That's the question, isn't it? But what we've got here, Mr. Kerlan, is a woman who threatened to run away, who may have had an affair, and, when she did finally leave, did not go anywhere logical, to family or a friend, or even to the man with whom she may have been having an affair—"

"I *told* you, there was no affair. You talked with Revell, didn't you say?"

"Oh, yes, he was very helpful. Told me just what you're telling me now. But what I'm thinking is that, if there was the *perception* of an affair, even for a time—"

"Detective Grant, I may be dense but I'm not *that* dense. Are you telling me you think I killed my wife?"

"Not at all!" Grant gave a falsely hearty laugh. "Did I say that?"

"Not in so many words. But the way you're talking . . ."

Another pause. "Let me put it this way, Mr. Kerlan. Usually when we have this kind of situation, a missing person the way we have here, a few logical possibilities usually present themselves. The most logical in this case is that your wife left and went to someone close to her. That hasn't happened. Another logical possibility is that she took off on a whim and went to a faraway place, on an airplane, perhaps, or a train or bus. Since she didn't take her car, this is the way we think. We've checked on this end as far as we could, and that doesn't seem to have happened. And if it had, usually after two or three days she would have contacted you or one of the other people close to her, to talk or just to let someone know she was all right. This is the kind of logic we use. After those two scenarios are excluded, there's another which often presents itself. That is, of course, that she never left at all. That she was . . ."

"Murdered. By me."

"Or someone else, Mr. Kerlan. Is there anyone else we should be looking at?"

"Could it have been a random thing, a serial killer?"

He had the feeling Grant almost laughed, but instead the detective said, "That's not a logical scenario at the moment, Mr. Kerlan. Like I said, is there anyone else . . . ?"

"No. Nobody I can think of."

"Then if you were me, and thinking logically . . ."

"You think I killed her. You think I went into a

jealous rage and murdered her, and hid her body, chopped it up with an ax, put it in a blender . . ."

Grant wasn't laughing on the other end of the line, and Kerlan suddenly realized the man might take him literally.

"I write horror fiction for a living, Detective."

"Yes, I know." The voice was a bit harder-edged.

"I didn't chop her up and put her in a blender."

Silence.

"Should we be talking further about this, Mr. Kerlan? With perhaps a lawyer present?"

"I didn't kill my wife, Detective."

Almost all of the civility was gone from Grant's voice. "Didn't you, Mr. Kerlan?"

"I didn't."

"Can you blame me for thinking such . . . well, horrible thoughts?"

"I can't, but you're wrong. If Ginny is dead, I didn't kill her."

"Do you think she's dead, Mr. Kerlan? After what I've said?"

His voice caught. "I don't know. I hope to God she isn't."

"I'll be in touch, Mr. Kerlan," Grant said, and there was an ominous note to his voice.

The line went dead.

Tomorrow, Peter thought, the previous night's dream coming into his head. *The one in the dream said I'd see her tomorrow.*

He worked the rest of the day and into evening in a fog. Two more complete Sam Hain outlines rolled across his monitor, along with sketches for three more that already begged for his attention. And all the while he heard the faintest of buzzings, going so far as to stop his feverish work at one point and make him search his office. But no matter where he searched the buzzing was faint and out of reach, and finally he went back to pounding the keys until exhaustion made him stop, with yet another moon, even fatter, rising across the window over his desk.

Without eating, he fell into bed and dreamed again of the black shrouded specter, the bleach-boned fingers gripping his shoulder, the whispering voice, dry as August in his ear: *Tomorrow. . . .*

CHAPTER TWELVE

He awoke.

Something was different. He noted a slight cooling in the air and saw with surprise that the sky was the deep sapphire blue of a true autumn day. The radio promised dropping temperatures all day, into the forties by dusk. Perfect fall weather.

Across the street the Meyer kids were busy, along with every other kid on the block. The streets and lawns were full of children suddenly possessed by the suddenly seasonal weather with mounting decorations, stringing pumpkin-shaped lights, transforming the neighborhood into the festival of orange and black it always became this time of year. Pumpkins seemed to have sprung up everywhere—not only on stoops and porches but in windows, perched on flower boxes, back decks, and, at one house, lined along the entire front of the house, an orange army guarding the lawn and fallen leaves. At the house next to the Meyers, a huge spiderweb of pale rope was being erected, pinned from the highest bare tree limb and reaching to the house's gutter, anchored in three places on the ground to make it stretch like a sail; two boys were hauling a huge and ugly black plastic spider from the garage to mount in its lair.

A steaming mug of coffee in his hand, Peter watched the frantic progress that would continue all day and culminate in a wonderland of Halloween by the time the moon replaced the sun.

He felt the first tendrils of cold weather coming and shivered for many reasons, then turned to go down to his office and work.

When he entered he heard insistent buzzing, and the chill down his spine broadened.

It's got to be in my mind.

He sat down before his monitor and began to work.

Another Sam Hain outline. And another. Sam and Holly on Mars. Sam and Holly Meet the Undergrounders. Sam and Holly and the Halloween Comet.

The buzzing wouldn't go away.

Morning melted into afternoon. Through the open casement window he heard shouts and laughter, and, finally, felt a cold breeze that deepened to the point where he had to close the window. For the first time since the previous winter, the house was chilly. Somewhere upstairs he heard the heat tick on.

Have to close those windows later.

At the casement window, leaves rattled against the screen, and something else bumped it and stayed.

A hornet.

He stared at it as another joined it, crawling, half flying, almost hopping, from the left of the window to cling to the screen.

What the . . .

The hornets, looking sluggish, crawled off, one of them making an attempt at flying before being blown back by the wind, clinging to the screen before dropping from sight.

He remembered what the beekeeper had said: that they would be active until the first cold spell, which would slow them down and then kill them off.

Another hornet appeared, and another.

With effort, he turned his mind back to the monitor and continued to work, pausing to bundle what he had done for the day and send it as an attachment to Revell. He was rewarded with an almost instantaneous return e-mail which effused: "Keep 'em comin', son! They love everything I've showed them so far! You'll be doing these wonderful things for the next ten years—THE KIDS WILL EAT THEM UP!"

He erased the message and went back to work.

In the back of his mind, like a growing hope, was the promise of the dream, that today he would see Ginny.

Please, he thought, *please let her come back.*

But the buzzing sound increased, becoming insistent, almost angry now. He paused once, thinking to do anything necessary to make it stop—rip the walls out, burn down the house, but the computer screen drew his eyes back:

Sam and Holly and the Texas Tornado.
Sam and Holly Meet the Leprechauns.

Sam and Holly and the Hornets of Doom.

He stopped, breathing hard, and stared at the screen.

That's it, he thought. *Enough.*

He pushed himself away from the desk, turned in his swivel chair and got unsteadily to his feet.

The buzzing sound was getting louder.

"Stop!" he shouted, putting his hands to his ears.

He pushed himself from the office, stumbled to the basement stairs, somehow dragged himself up to the main floor.

The house was dark and cold, and suffused only by orange light from outside.

For a moment he was disoriented. Then he remembered the frantic neighborhood activity of the day.

He staggered to a window, closed it and looked out.

A wonderland of orange met his eyes.

The lights in the neighborhood had been lit— strings of them in trees and across gutters and around door frames, orange and white. And pumpkins were everywhere, as if the town had turned a single color. As he closed another window he could almost smell the way they would become in a few weeks, their scooped insides sweet-cold and wet, the smell of whispered cinnamon, allspice.

For a moment he was lost in the smell and lights, and tears ran down his face and he was cold and helpless.

Ginny, come back to me!

Through the window he noticed a car parked in front of his house.

A curl of cigarette smoke rose from the open window on the driver's side, and he saw the man sitting there looking his way now and then.

It looked like Detective Grant, but he couldn't be sure, until the man tilted what looked like a flask to his mouth.

Go to hell, you bastard.

The night grew colder, more blustery; leaves began to dance around the lawn like dervishes.

Then, abruptly, it was quiet. The wind ceased. The car in front of Kerlan's house remained, along with the curl of smoke.

Some of the strung pumpkin lights went out, leaving the block more eerie.

Kerlan locked the front door, closed the remaining windows, found a sweater in his bedroom and went back down to his office.

It was cold inside—and was filled with the sound of buzzing.

When he stepped into the room, his foot crushed something alive and wriggling on the carpet.

A hornet.

Others were moving over the rug, crawling slowly up the walls from behind the couch; one made a feeble try at flying up toward the light but fell back, exhausted, to land on the coffee table, which held manuscripts in front of the sofa.

"What in God's name?"

He ran to his office phone, rifled through the stacks of papers on his desk, looking for the phone number of Willims, the beekeeper.

A hornet was crawling tiredly across the front edge of the desk, and he swatted it angrily to the floor.

There were more yellow jackets, scores of them, moving toward the desk from the far end of the office, more climbing up the walls.

He found the number, punched keys, waiting impatiently.

Be there, dammit!

A sleepy voice answered the phone and yawned "Hello?"

Peter identified himself and almost shouted into the receiver, "They're back, dammit! All over the place! What the hell is going on?"

The beekeeper yawned again. "Fell asleep in front of the TV," he explained. "Watching *Frankenstein Meets the Wolfman*. Good flick." He laughed. Another, more drawn out yawn. "You say they came back? Impossible. We killed that nest dead."

"Then what the hell is happening?"

A pause. "Only thing I can think of is that there was a second nest, like I mentioned to you. Real unusual, but it does happen. Two females, probably from the same brood originally, established nests near each other. This ain't the original nest we're talking about, but a whole new one. Wow. Haven't seen this in a long time."

"Can you get rid of it?"

"Sure. What's probably happening now is the cold is killing off the drones. You must have missed a spot in the baseboard, and they're being driven from the nest to the light and heat in your office. Why don't you look for the opening in the baseboard while I get over there—plug that up with tape and that'll take care of your office. Then we'll find the new nest and knock 'em out in no time. They're on the way out anyway." He laughed shortly, giving a half yawn. "Wow. Two nests. That's somethin'."

"Just get over here!"

Peter slammed down the phone and went to the sofa. He moved the coffee table in front of it, then angled the couch out, away from the wall.

A mass of sluggish hornets were clustered on the rug in front of a gap in the baseboard.

More in anger than in fright, he grabbed a wad of papers from the coffee table, rolled them into a makeshift tube and cleared the front of the opening of hornets. They moved willingly. He ran back to his desk, retrieved a length of cellophane tape, and with a practiced motion wadded it as he went back to the baseboard.

Already another hornet, followed by yet another sluggish insect, was crawling through the space.

Peter thrust the wadded cellophane at the opening, pushing the two new intruders backward as the hole was plugged.

The sound of buzzing was very loud behind the wall.

And now, being this close to the wall, he noticed another sound—a rustling movement, a thin sound, as if someone were scratching weakly against the other side of the wall.

And then a pained, tepid whisper: "*Peter. . . .*"

"What—"

He stood up, brushing a few slow-crawling hornets from the wall and put his ear flush against it.

It came again, the thinnest of rustling breaths heard behind a thick chorus of buzzing: *"Peter, help me. . . ."*

"*Ginny!*" he shouted.

"*Yes. . . ."*

"My God—"

"*Peter. . . ."*

He drew back from the wall, balling his fists as if he would smash through it—then he turned, throwing open the office door and dashing through and up the stairs. He ran for the back sliding door, nearly tripping over Ginny's things in the hallway, his mind feverish.

"My God, Ginny . . ."

He pushed himself out into the now cold night, a full October chill hitting his face as he shouted, "Ginny!"

The backyard was lit by the sharp circle of the moon, by a few orange and white lights still lit in houses behind his, visible through denuded oaks.

"Ginny, where are you?"

He heard a rustle to his right, against the house, in darkness.

He stumbled down the back deck steps.

"Ginny!"

"Here, Peter, help me. . . ."

Breathing heavily, he found himself standing before the garden shed, its bulk looming in front of him. The sound of buzzing was furious, caught in the cold wind.

"Peter . . ."

He screamed, an inarticulate sound, and pulled at the shed's door, which wouldn't budge.

My God, she must have been caught inside the shed. The door must have closed on her and trapped her inside!

His mind filled with roiling thoughts. He pulled and clawed and banged at the door, trying to open it.

"Help me please, Peter. . . ."

"Jesus!" The door wouldn't move. He looked wildly around for a tool, something to pry it open with—and then spied the short handle of a spade lying close by on the grass.

He picked it up, noting faint scratches on the spade's face—this must have been how Ginny had gotten the door open originally.

"Peter . . ."

"I'm coming!"

Mad with purpose, he pried the spade into the thin opening between wooden door and jamb, beginning to work it back. There was a creaking sound, but the door held firm.

"Dammit!"

"Peter, please . . ."

He hammered on the handle of the spade, driving it deeper into the opening. He angled it sideways and suddenly the wooden handle broke away, leaving him with the metal arm that had been imbedded in it attached to the blade. He pushed at the blade, getting faint purchase but shouting with the effort.

"Dammit!" The handle slipped, slicing into his hand, but he ignored the pain, the quick line of blood, and kept pushing and banging.

The door gave a bit, but still wouldn't open.

Buzzing filled his ears, an angry sound now—he realized that when he opened the door the hornets might rush out at him, but he didn't care. He drove the thought from his mind.

"Peter . . ."

The voice was growing fainter.

He shouted, and became aware that lights were going on around him—still, he beat at the handle.

The door gave way another fraction; it was almost open . . .

"Jesus! Open, dammit!"

With a supreme effort that caused the broken metal handle of the spade to push painfully into his open wound, the door opened with a huge groaning creak and flew back on its hinges.

"Ginny!"

"Peter . . ."

There was darkness within, a seething fog of flying things—and then something stumbled out into his arms, something white and alive, a human skeleton with a skin made of hornets. Writhing orange and black insects covered her skull, her arms, her fingers, which gripped him tightly as he stumbled backward screaming in its embrace. The thing walked with him, holding him tightly, hornets all over Ginny's face, boiling alive in the empty eye sockets to make eyes and hair and lips on the skeletal mouth.

The mouth moved, the opening jawbone hissing with the movement of hornets. The writhing face showed something that was almost tenderness.

"Kiss me, Peter. Kiss me . . ."

He screamed, pushing at the thing, which would not let him go, aware suddenly that there were others nearby. He turned his head to see Detective Grant and Willims standing side-by-side, rooted by horror to the spot they stood in, flashlights trained on him.

"Kiss me, Peter. Samhain let me come back. The Lord of the Dead let me come back, but only for a little while. I never stopped loving you. . . ."

The thing covered in hornets turned and looked straight at Detective Grant. There was a sudden hard look to the writhing features.

"Samhain says something is coming. He says stay out of it. If you don't, he will kill your wife and everyone close to you."

And now Peter felt the first stings as the hornets began to peel away from Ginny's skeleton, covering his own face, attacking him—

"Help me!" he screamed.

Ginny melted away in his arms, the bones collapsing in a clacking pile as Peter fell to the ground, covered in angry hornets. Through his burning eyes he saw the beekeeper standing over him, wide-eyed, waving his arms, his flashlight beam bouncing, shouting something that Peter could no longer hear through his swollen ears, his screaming mouth filled with soft angry hornets, his throat, his body covered inside his clothing.

He gave a horrid final choking scream and was silent.

CHAPTER THIRTEEN

"And that's the way you'd like the record to read?" District Attorney Morton said. He was shaking his head as he said it—but then again, he had been shaking his head since the informal inquest had begun two hours ago.

Detective Grant spoke up. "This will be sealed, right?"

Morton laughed shortly, a not humorous sound. "You bet your ass it will be. We're lucky nobody from the press got wind of this." He looked sideways at the beekeeper. "We're not going to have any trouble from you, are we, Mr. Willims?"

The beekeeper nearly gulped. "Are you kidding? If Detective Grant hadn't been standing next to me, do you think the bunch of you would even be listening to me? I'd be in a looney bungalow right now." He turned to face Grant. "Tell them what that thing told you. The message from Samhain it gave you."

Tight-lipped, Grant said nothing.

Morton kept his eyes on Willims. "Yes, Mr. Willims, without Detective Grant you would now be in a straitjacket. Especially since you're the only one making all these claims about 'Samhain' and such. But since the two of you saw this strange killing take place . . ."

The beekeeper gulped again, and Grant nodded curtly.

"At least I don't think Kerlan killed his wife," Grant said. "It looks to me like she got herself stuck in that gardening shed, and the hornets got to her." He looked at Willims, and suddenly everyone was looking at the beekeeper.

"You want me to tell you this all could happen? Sure, I'll tell you—but I still don't believe it. Could hornets strip a human body clean in a few days? Well, maybe. Usually hornets won't eat human flesh, but if the opportunity presents itself, I guess they might. They probably stung her to death after she got trapped in the shed. And then the body was in there with them . . . so, sure, I guess it could happen."

"And what about the supposed . . ."—Morton consulted the papers before him—". . . mobility of the skeleton . . . ?" He let the question hang, and Grant finally spoke up.

"The damn thing looked like it stumbled out of the shed. But it could have been a trick of the light. If the skeletal remains had been propped against the door when Kerlan opened it, which would have been consistent with his wife's trying to get out of the shed until she was overcome by the hornets, then, sure, it could have tumbled out into his arms."

He looked over at the beekeeper, who looked at his shoes. "Yeah, I guess that's what I saw, too."

Morton addressed the beekeeper: "And the bees covering Mrs. Kerlan like skin—that could have been a 'trick of the light' too?"

"Well . . ."

Willims looked up from his shoes to see Grant glaring at him.

"Sure, I guess so. And I guess the words we heard her say could have been in our minds. . . ."

For a moment he looked defiant before collapsing. "All right. It was all in our heads."

"Fine," Morton said. He had gained a satisfied look. He turned to the medical examiner. "Hank, you're okay with the cause of death in both cases as being extreme toxic reaction to hornet stings?"

The ME nodded once. "Yep."

"And there was nothing the two of you could have done to save him?" he asked Grant and Willims.

The beekeeper said, "By the time we got to him he'd already been stung hundreds of times. I was able to get some of them off, but it was too late. The weirdest thing is that they wouldn't respond to light, which threw me. When I shined my flashlight on them they should have flocked to it."

"But they could have been so angry at that point that they would have ignored the light, correct?" Morton said sharply.

"I guess so. But I still say they should have attacked the light and left Mr. Kerlan alone."

"But you're fine with the way we wrote it up in the final report?" Morton said, daring the beekeeper to contradict him.

"Yes, I suppose so."

"Good. Anything else?" Morton patted his knees, making as if to rise, daring anyone in the room not to let him end the proceedings.

There was a glum silence. Once again the beekeeper was staring at his own shoes.

"I want to reemphasize, Mr. Willims, that you aren't to speak to anyone of what went on in here today. We're all sworn to secrecy. This record *will* be sealed. Whatever was said in this room remains in this room. I don't want to see anything in the newspapers about humans made out of yellow jackets or . . ."—here he consulted his notes again—". . . Samhain, the Lord of the Dead. You understand?"

Without lifting his gaze, Willims answered, "Sure."

Letting a hard edge climb into his tone, Morton said, "If any of this finds its way into the press, or anywhere else outside this room, I'll know who to call on, won't I, Mr. Willims?"

The beekeeper nodded. His gaze shifted momentarily to Grant, whose face was blank.

"Just so you understand," Morton continued, "there are licenses and such in your profession, and I would hate for you to have trouble in that area."

The beekeeper nodded again.

Morton's tone switched suddenly from hard to hearty. "All right, then—that's it!" He stood and stretched, glancing at the ME. "Hank—lunch?"

"Yep," the ME said.

The rest of them rose, and as Grant passed Willims he leaned close and whispered sharply, "We both know what really happened. I'll take care of it."

On the way out of the room the district attorney put his arm briefly around the beekeeper's shoulder and said, "Just forget about it, Willims. Chalk it up to professional strangeness."

Willims looked up at the DA, and for a moment his face was haunted.

"The thing I can't get over," he said, "is the stuff she was saying about the Lord of the Dead, how she'd been brought back from the dead."

Morton's scowl turned to an angry frown. "I warned you in there, Willims—"

"I heard you," the beekeeper said resignedly. "Believe me, I heard you."

Morton removed his arm from the other man's shoulder, giving him a slight shove forward. "Just don't forget what I said."

They were in the marbled hallway of the court building leading toward the revolving doors to the outside world. Morton watched Willims go through them, slouching with unhappiness.

The ME came up behind Morton and tapped him on the shoulder.

"Meet you at the restaurant," he said laconically. "I've got to dip into my office upstairs for a minute."

"Fine."

The ME peeled off into another hallway, his footsteps echoing away on the polished stone floor.

After a moment, the DA composed himself into his public face of smiling bluster and strode through the revolving doors.

Outside it was cold and bright, early November chill making the recent October heat wave a memory.

The DA shivered, wishing he had remembered his topcoat. But the restaurant was only a block away.

He had began to descend the wide stone steps of the courthouse that led to the street when something small and striped orange and black, an insect, brushed by his ear and settled lightly there.

He heard the faintest of whispers before he swatted it away—as if someone were talking to him from a far distance. Later, until the voice came again and he was sure, he would wonder if he had heard it at all:

"I may want you to do something for me. . . ."

PART II

FALSE LEADS

CHAPTER FOURTEEN

Perhaps it was the wind that first brought him to the town of Orangefield, a wind that made leaf tornados, dervishing colors from denuded trees. Or perhaps it was the chill in the air, the first cold tendrils of coming winter that were autumn. Or perhaps it was the children bedecked in their autumn sweaters—or the windows with cutouts, or the pumpkins, wet and cold and sweet inside, orange, firm and smiling on the outside. Or the season, or the fact that the town had briefly been called Pumpkinfield.

Or perhaps it was because he needed somewhere to serve his master.

Or maybe it was the special evening that would soon be here.

His evening.

There are many ways to skin a cat.

"Yes," the other voice answered. "Indeed. But I am becoming tired of your failed efforts."

This Halloween will be different. I feel the power within me for this. This time I will succeed.

"And then?" the other voice asked.

And then everything. And I will give it over to you, Dark One.

"Do you really think you can do it directly? Without passing through that . . . other place?"

I feel powerful. As powerful as ever.

"You've said this before."

This time I have three sure ones to help me. The girl Wizard and two others. And . . .

"And?"

I have what you might call . . . insurance.

"But if, like the last time, one of them fails . . ."

Everything will succeed.

"We shall see."

There is only one problem, and it will be solved soon. This man Grant, this detective, there is something about him . . .

"You can handle him?"

Not in the usual way. He is one of the strong ones, unlike Kerlan, who was disrespectful and weak. Grant must be pushed aside.

"Do it, then."

It will be done. I am only your servant.

"True words. A servant without a choice. I will watch your progress with interest, Samhain." The voice laughed, a mirthless sound as cold and dead as space. "Or should I call you Sam?"

CHAPTER FIFTEEN

Jody Wendt, five years old, saw the Pumpkin Boy through the window over the kitchen sink, outlined against the huge rising moon like a silhouette against a white screen. Jody had climbed up onto the counter next to the basin to reach the cereal in an overhead cabinet. Now he stood transfixed with a box of corn flakes in his hands, mouth agape.

The Pumpkin Boy had a bright orange pumpkin head with cold night steam puffing out of the eyes, nose and mouth cutouts, and a body consisting of a bright metal barrel chest and jointed legs and arms that looked like stainless steel rails. Even through the closed window Jody could hear the creaking noises he made. He moved stiffly, like he was unused to walking; his feet were two flat ovoid pads, slightly rounded and raised on top, made of shiny metal. As Jody watched, one of the feet stuck in place in the muddy ground; the Pumpkin Boy, oblivious, walked on, and then toppled over with a sound like rusting machinery. He lay on the ground like a turtle on its back, making a hollow chuffing noise like *saaaafe, saaaafe, saaaafe*. Then he slowly righted himself, rising to a sitting position and then turned slowly to search for his lost foot. Finding it, he fell forward and clawed his way toward it. He closed his hands around it. His head fell forward and hit the ground, rolling away from the body, and the hands immediately let go of the foot and grabbed the head, realigning it on the stilt body with a *ffffffmp*.

Then the foot was reattached to the leg and the Pumpkin Boy stood up with a groaning, complaining metal sound.

The Pumpkin Boy reached back down, creaking loudly, to pluck two fat organic pumpkins from Mr. Schwartz's field, which grew behind Jody's yard, and began to move off, away into the night.

"*Wow* . . . ," Jody whispered against the window pane, making it fog. He quickly cleared it with the cuff of his shirt and watched the Pumpkin Boy stiffly climb the fence that bordered Mr. Schwartz's pumpkin patch from another behind it. In the process the Pumpkin Boy lost hold of one of the pumpkins he held but paid no heed.

"*Wow* . . . ," Jody whispered again.

Jody was alone in the house; it was the half hour in between the time when the afternoon sitter left and his mother came home from her job in town.

He had been told repeatedly that he was not to leave the house during that in-between time.

The forgotten box of corn flakes lay spilling cereal

into the kitchen sink as he climbed down, pushed his arms into his jacket and opened the door, which led from the kitchen to the backyard.

As Jody Wendt stood on the top step of the back stoop, the storm door closing with a *hiss* and *bang* behind him, he saw the Pumpkin Boy once again outlined against the moon, but moving quickly away. He was already two fields over, and would soon drop behind the slope that led down to Martin's Creek and the valley beyond.

Mouth still open in amazement, Jody was working at the zipper to his jacket, which wouldn't zip. His feet were already carrying him down the steps, across the yard, to the split-log fence.

He dipped under the fence, forgetting the zipper, and stood in Mr. Schwartz's pumpkin patch on the other side.

The Pumpkin Boy's head was just visible, and then the slope down made him disappear.

Jody hurried on.

Mr. Schwartz's pumpkin field was furrowed, bursting with fat vined pumpkins ready to be picked and sold for Halloween. Jody tripped over the first row he came to and landed on his hands.

He found himself face-to-face with a huge oval orange fruit, its skin hard and strong.

It looked like a human head.

Jody pushed himself up and stumbled on.

He fell twice more. But still, in the distance, he could hear the metallic creaking sounds of the Pumpkin Boy. There were two more fences to manage, another one of split logs, which Jody scooted under, and the other of chain link, which he climbed with difficulty.

He nearly toppled over when he reached the top, but then, in the distance, he saw an orange flash in the moonlight—the top of the Pumpkin Boy's head. He held on and descended to the other side.

There was a rock wall, which Jody had never known existed, separating two more pumpkin fields.

Jody was now in unfamiliar territory. From his bedroom window, just before harvest, the fields surrounding his house were awash in taut orange fruit, and now, for the first time, he knew just how complicated the layout was.

At yet another rock wall he paused to look back. He could no longer see his house.

He heard a sharp metallic creak in the far distance and hurried toward it.

The pumpkin field ended in a tangle of weeds and brambles and a ledge. Abruptly, Jody found himself teetering at the top of the slope. A tuft of brambles caught his foot and twisted his ankle and, with a short surprised gasp, he was tumbling down the damp, soft bank.

At the bottom, he came up against an uprooted oak trunk, coming to a stop with one of its gnarled roots pointing into his face like an accusing finger.

He sat up, soiled and wet.

Suddenly, he realized what he had done.

He looked back up the slope and shuddered with the thought that, even if he could climb the steep incline, he would not be able to find his way back home through the tangle of pumpkin fields.

A quick, hot shiver of fear shot up his back.

But then, in front of him, like the sound of the Pied Piper's flute, there came the creaking sound of the Pumpkin Boy moving. The pumpkin head flashed through the trees, and Jody forgot his fear. His wonder renewed, he stood and ran after it.

The moon was partially hidden by a thick tangle of trees on the far bank of Martin's Creek, which made shafts of gray-white light on the ground. Jody splashed into the creek before he knew it was in front of him. His hurt foot slid down into icy tumbling water and lodged between two rocks.

Jody cried out in pain. For a moment he couldn't move, and panicked—but then, suddenly, one of the stones upended in the water and rolled over, and he was free.

Now both sneakers were in the water, and the slight current tugged at his legs.

He tried to turn around, but the water hurried him out farther.

He sank another half foot into the water.

The current was trying to make him sit down, which would bring his head underwater.

He gave a weak cry as he lost his struggle, and then there was water in his mouth and he could see nothing but the blur of moving wetness.

Almost immediately, his body pressed up against something long, dark and solid, and his forward progress stopped.

It was a half-submerged log.

Jody clung to it and slowly pulled himself up.

To his surprise, the creek was only about two feet deep here. The whooshing sound of water angrily churning around the log filled his ears.

He held onto the dry part of the log and coughed water out.

He wiped his eyes with one hand, and then had another surprise: not only was the water shallow, it was not half as wide as it had been just a few yards upstream.

Holding the log, he pushed his way through the shallow water to the far bank.

He sat down and his eyes filled with tears.

I want to go home, he thought.

He stared out at totally unfamiliar territory. The creek, he now saw, twisted and turned, and he could not make out the spot where he had descended the slope, which was nearly a hundred yards away, and impossibly wide. At the top of the ridge, reflected in moonlight, were the green-vined tops of a few elongated pumpkins.

He turned and saw that the line of woods was close, and darker than it had looked from the other side of the creek.

The trees were nearly nude, a carpet of yellow and red fallen leaves at their bases looking light and dark gray in the moonlight.

A few late leaves pirouetted down as he watched.

Deep in the woods, he heard the Pumpkin Boy move.

Jody looked once again behind him, and then back at the woods.

He got up painfully and hobbled toward the trees.

* * *

It instantly became darker when he entered the woods—a grayer, more sporadic light.

Almost immediately, Jody lost his bearings.

There were many strange noises that confused him. He thought he heard the Pumpkin Boy nearby, but the sound proved to be a partially broken oak branch, creaking in the wind. There were rustlings and stirrings. Something on four legs scuttled past him in the near distance, and stopped to stare at him—it looked like a red fox, bleached gray by the night.

Jody tried to retrace his steps, but only found himself deeper within the trees, which now all looked the same.

Jody's ankle hurt, and he was beginning to shiver.

He stopped, even hushing his own frightened breathing, and listened for the Pumpkin Boy. The sound of the Pumpkin Boy's movement was completely gone.

A soft wind had arisen, and now leaves lifted from the forest floor, as if jerked alive by puppet strings. It had turned colder—above, the moon was abruptly shielded by a gust of clouds. The woods became very dark.

Jody sobbed again, stumbling forward, and stopped in a small clearing surrounded by tall oaks. Again he heard scurrying in front of him and felt something watching him.

The moon blinked out of the clouds, and Jody saw that it was indeed a red fox, regarding him with wary interest. The fox became suddenly alert. As the moon's nightlight was stolen again by clouds, the animal bolted away, seeming to jump into the darkness.

Jody stood rooted to his spot, trying not to cry.

Something was out there.

Something large and dark.

The bed of leaves shifted with heavy, creaking steps.

Something ice-cold and long and thin brushed along his face in the darkness.

"I want to go home!" Jody blurted out in fear and despair.

The cold air was suddenly steamed with warmth.

Cold braces closed around Jody's middle from behind. He shrieked and wrenched his body around.

He was blinded by something larger and brighter than the moon—a face staring down at him made out of a jack-o'-lantern, warm wet fog pushing from its triangular eyes and nose and impossibly wide, smiling mouth. A slight mechanical *chuff* issued along with the sour, oily-smelling steam.

The slender mechanical steel arms tightened around Jody.

He shrieked again, a mournful sound swallowed by the trees and close night around him.

As he was carried away he saw, as the moon broke forth from the clouds again, on the forest floor, caught in gray light, the smashed leavings of a dropped pumpkin.

CHAPTER SIXTEEN

Another damn Halloween.

Len Schneider was beginning to work up a deep and real hatred for holidays in general, and this one especially. Halloween, he knew, meant nothing but trouble. He'd moved to Orangefield for lots of reasons, among them the fact that it had a genuine small-town feel. It was only place he'd lived in the last twenty years that didn't have a Wal-Mart and wasn't likely to get one. The people seemed friendly enough, but as a police detective he'd found that people were pretty much the same everywhere, from the inner city to Hometown, U.S.A. "People are funny," Art Linkletter used to say, and one thing Len Schneider had learned after eighteen years in law enforcement was that they were anything but.

And now this *thing* came along—the thing he'd left Milwaukee to get away from. . . .

"When was the last time you had a missing kid

case?" he'd asked Bill Grant, the other detective on Orangefield's police force. Grant had been at it a long time, too, but all of it in this town. In the year and a half Schneider had been here, he'd found Grant polite but almost aloof. No, aloof wasn't the right word—it was almost like he wasn't completely there. The two packs of cigarettes a day he smoked didn't seem to help, and the emphysemic cough that went along with them, along with the booze he drank, had turned him almost sickly.

Schneider thought he was haunted himself, by what had happened back in Milwaukee, but this guy was even worse.

He'd tried to get Grant to open up a few times, once over a bottle of Scotch, but all that had happened was that he'd opened up himself, letting his own bile and anger out. He wondered if Grant even remembered, though he had a feeling he did. Behind the hollows of those eyes the cop mind still worked, and Schneider had been told that Grant was very good at his job.

But Grant had *really* gotten weird after a case a week ago involving a local children's book author, Peter Kerlan. Something about both Kerlan and his wife being killed by insects. . . .

Grant was leaning back in his chair, his fingers idly drumming the neatly arranged desk in front of him. The man's skin looked almost jaundiced. Just as Schneider was about to repeat his question, Grant said, without moving his eyes or head, "We've had a few over the years. They almost always turn up."

"Ever anything in Orangefield . . ."

"Like yours in Milwaukee?" Grant almost

snapped. The confirmation that Grant not only remembered the night of Scotch, but had also absorbed and catalogued everything that had gone on, startled Schneider.

"Yes, like mine in Milwaukee," Schneider replied evenly.

"Not unless you go back a long way. Long before you or me."

Schneider waited for elaboration, but there was none.

"Any chance you'd like to give me this one?" Grant said.

Another silence hung between them, and then Schneider replied, "None."

Schneider was swiveling toward his own desk when he caught Grant leaning forward, his eyes finally giving him attention. He swiveled back, his hands on his knees.

Grant was staring at him, a bit too intently. His yellow fingers had stopped drumming and lay perfectly still on his desk blotter. Schneider suddenly saw the intelligence in the sunken light blue eyes.

"I know you want to make good on what happened in Milwaukee," Grant said carefully. For the first time his gaze fell on Schneider as something more than a concept—Grant was actually *looking* at him. "I don't blame you. It's just that this one has that . . . aura around it. Like the one last week."

"You mean the Kerlan deaths—"

"Yes," Grant shot back. "Around this time of year weird things always happen in Orangefield, but this is different. And I want to find out why."

"The Wendt case is mine," Schneider said with finality. He moved to swivel back to his desk, but Grant's eyes held him.

"There are worse things than a missing kid," Grant said.

Sudden anger flared in Schneider, but he saw that Grant seemed to be looking inward, not at him anymore.

Grant seemed to catch himself, and his sallow neck actually reddened. He fumbled with the small notebook on his desk, opened and closed it.

"I'm sorry, Len," Grant said, his voice lowered almost to a whisper. "I can imagine what that case of yours was like in Milwaukee. That kid's parents, especially his father going insane. He was some kind of genius or something, right?" He shook his head slowly from side to side; the flush of color had left his features. "There are some things you never forget. Sometimes I think about myself too much. . . ." For a brief moment his neck reddened again. "Sorry."

Then Grant leaned back in his chair again, his fingers drumming lightly on the neat desk.

The interview was over.

There are worse things than a missing kid. . . .

"No, there aren't," Len Schneider said to himself, loud enough for someone else to hear.

CHAPTER SEVENTEEN

The kid might have been eleven or twelve. Without a face, it was hard to tell if he had been good-looking or not—sometimes by that age, you can tell how the features will set through the teen years. He looked like he was sleeping when they dug him up—his hand resting under his head, the face, or where the face would have been, was turned into the dirt so that it looked like he had nuzzled into a pillow. The hand was covering a ragged hole in the boy's head where his brains had literally been beaten in. He was still fully clothed, except for his shoes and socks—later they found that he had been undressed and then redressed by Carlton, who had kept the footwear, along with one of the boy's toes, as souvenirs.

Jerry Carlton had almost boasted about it at his trial—his shaggy hair had been cut and combed, his red tie knotted, his eyes covered with mirrored sunglasses which, thank God, the judge had made him remove. He smiled through the whole proceeding, and played with his watch.

He could fix a tractor, a television set, could build just about anything, and had murdered five boys in three states calling himself Carlton the Clown. He'd worn a different clown costume for each murder.

Len had never forgotten that: Carlton the Clown.

He'd wanted only three minutes alone with Jerry Carlton, but they wouldn't give it to him.

Just three minutes . . .

And nearly every night, because he made a mistake, Len Schneider dreamed of a kid with no face, turning his head from where it was nuzzled into his pillow and staring at him with empty eye sockets, trying to speak without lips. . . .

This time, Len Schneider vowed to himself, he'd get his three minutes.

And he wouldn't make any mistakes.

CHAPTER EIGHTEEN

Schneider was convinced the Wendt kid was not merely missing. Everything pointed to it. The kid's mother (another thing that made it worse—there was no father, he had died in a construction accident four years ago) swore her son had never left the house by himself before. Which led Schneider at first to conventional lines: that whoever had taken the child had learned the house routine and knew that there was a window of opportunity every once in a while when the child was alone for a half hour, between his afternoon sitter leaving and his mother getting home from work.

But there were no signs of forced entry, which led Len automatically to the next line of enquiry: that the child had unlocked the back door himself and let the abductor in.

Which could have happened—although, again, there was no evidence that anyone had been in the house. It had been a quick snatch, if that had been the case, which meant that the boy had probably known the assailant.

Which was possible, up to a point—the point being a weird one. It had rained most of the week before the abduction, and because of that and the recent freak autumn heat wave that had prevented the ground from getting cold and hard, the ground had been fairly soft; but there was only one set of footprints in the backyard leading away from the house to the back fence.

This indicated that someone had lured him over the fence—*something he had never done before*—without actually stepping into the backyard himself.

When he asked Mrs. Wendt for a list of people, with the emphasis on males, who might be enough of authority figures in her son Jody's eyes to entice him to do such a thing, her face went blank. There were no clergy, no relatives, no real male role model who he would follow over that fence, she was sure.

He told her to think about it, and if anyone came to her to let him know right away.

At that point Schneider did the conventional thing: he followed the child's footprints as far as he could. And it was quite a job: behind the Wendt property was a patchwork quilt of pumpkin fields owned by various farmers. He nonetheless was able to follow the boy's movements through four of these fields to the edge of a fifth, which then dropped off down to a shallow valley and a thin ribbon of water known as Martin's Creek.

From the marks he found, it looked as though the boy had slid or fallen down the embankment. There were indications that he had crossed the creek.

For a moment, Schneider's heart climbed into his throat when he saw how deep the creek was at the point the boy entered. He followed the line of water downstream, fearing that the boy's drowned body might turn up at any moment. But he found markings on the other side of the water at a shallower area where a fallen tree bridged the creek (perhaps the boy *was* in trouble until he came up against this spot) and these fresh marks led into the tangle of trees on the other side of the water.

The odd thing was that there were only the boy's tracks. He broadened his search and discovered that a second, oddly shaped set of tracks led from the pumpkin field behind the Wendt house down the embankment into the woods, but they were nowhere near the boy's. This led him to believe that, perhaps, the boy had been *following* someone.

Out of breath and sweating a little, his slight paunch only one indication of how out of shape he was (*thirty years old and already starting to look like an old cop*), he found himself at a spot in the patch of woods marked by a broken pumpkin, where both sets of tracks converged.

It was here, obviously, that the boy was abducted.

There were signs of a struggle. And then only the second set of prints—which were very odd indeed, not shoe or boot prints but large flat ovoids, which made him think that someone had worn some sort

of covering over his shoes to disguise the prints—
led away.

And then, abruptly, in the middle of nowhere,
among a gloomy stand of gnarled trees, so thick and
twisted they blocked all light from above, they
stopped.

At that point the hair on the back of Schneider's
head (where there still *was* hair, a good part of the
top of his head being bald) stood on end. He looked
at the clearing he stood in, covered with leaves and
dead branches.

Where . . .

He brought in dogs, of course, and along with two
uniformed policemen he brushed the area of leaves
and twigs, looking for an underground opening. But
there was none. Even the dogs, who had been given
a piece of Jody Wendt's clothing, had stopped at the
same spot Schneider had.

One of them threw back its head and bayed,
which, again, made the hair on the back of Schneider's head stand on end.

Jody Wendt had disappeared into thin air.

CHAPTER NINETEEN

The poster, which read: UNCLE LOLLIPOP LOVES YOU!
was upside down. He was glad his mom had taught
him to read. There was more writing at the bottom of
the poster, but he couldn't make out what it said because it was too small and it was also upside down.
So was everything else. The sign was in bright colors, red and blue and yellow and green, as if the colors had been splashed on or finger painted—they
ran over their borders and looked still wet. The room
smelled like paint, like the time his mother had
painted his bedroom in March and left all the windows open. He'd slept on the couch in the living
room that night (sneaking the television on at three
in the morning, but there had only been commercials on for exercise equipment—some of which his
mom had—and for calcium and vitamin supplements, so he had soon tired and turned the TV off)

and when he went back to his room the next night he got sick to his stomach, even though the paint was dry and the windows had been left open a crack. A week later all his own posters and his bookshelf with *Mike Mulligan and His Steam Shovel* (his favorite book) and *The Wizard of Oz* were back, and the smell was gone. He'd forgotten his room had ever been painted.

But the smell wasn't gone here—it was stronger. It had a curious burning odor underneath the paint smell, as if someone was heating paint in a pan.

That was funny, heating paint in a pan . . .

He felt light-headed, and suddenly wanted to throw up.

Ahhhhh . . .

The discomforting noise he made caused another noise outside of his vision, a shuffling like a dog had been disturbed. He could not see anything except for the upside down poster and an upside down coat hook next to it with a raincoat that was hung near the floor and ran up the wall (again: funny! And despite his queasy stomach he gurgled a short laugh). The wall was colored chocolate brown, and it was stuffy in the room.

Again he heard the shuffling sound.

Something new came into his view, in front of the wall poster—something just as brightly colored. It was accompanied by the shuffling noise, which was caused, Jody saw, when he strained his eyes to look up (which hurt) by the slow movement of a pair of huge clown feet, which were red with bright yellow laces. His vision in that direction was impeded by a sort of cap that appeared to be on his head, though he felt nothing there. There was a sharp rim, and he could see no farther. What he saw of the ceiling under the clown's feet was the same color as the wall.

Jody looked down, and his sight trailed over the figure of a circus clown dressed in blue pants, a red and green-striped blouse with baggy sleeves and white gloves, and a white face with an impossibly wide, bright red smile and eyelashes painted all around his eyes, all topped by a snow-white cap with a red pom-pom.

The shuffling stopped; the clown was facing him now and Jody noted that the figure's real lips inside the painted on smile weren't smiling. The eyes looked serious inside their cartoon lashes, too.

"Ted?" the clown whispered in an impossibly gentle voice. "You're awake, Ted?"

Jody tried to tell the clown that his name wasn't Ted, but the feared throw-up rose hotly in his throat, out his mouth and ran up his face.

It was now, through the paint smell and dizziness and headache, that he realized *he* was upside down, not the room.

The clown *tsk-tsk*ed, and a wet cloth was pressed to Jody's nose and cheeks, rubbed gently.

The bile was gone.

It was getting very stuffy in the room.

"Soon, Ted, soon . . . ," the clown said, and then he shuffled out of Jody's sight.

"I—" Jody managed to get out.

The shuffling stopped. "Yes?" the clown asked, and there was a closed-in hush in the room.

"I ... no ... Ted ...," Jody spit out, along with more bile, before his vision began to blur.

"I know, Ted. Yes," the clown answered, in what was almost a singsong whisper.

Then Jody closed his eyes.

When he opened them again, he was hungry.

The paint smell was still there, and the queasiness, and the headache, which was worse now, and he was still upside down and couldn't move. But, somehow, he felt more alert.

He saw immediately that the poster—UNCLE LOL-LIPOP LOVES YOU!—was partially blocked by a familiar sight: the Pumpkin Boy, or at least part of him. The Pumpkin Boy's chest, which was a thicker tube of metal than the articulated stalks that composed his arms, was open, revealing a cavity within with something red, suspended in a web of golden wire, that throbbed darkly. The web shivered noticeably with each beat. The cavity's door was hinged against the Pumpkin Boy's side. He seemed to be missing from the legs down (or up, to Jody's eyes) and his head was flipped open on the top. Now, in the light, Jody saw that the head itself looked to be made of some sort of ceramic or plastic or other hard material; it was too hard-edged and brightly colored (a hue as bright as the poster colors and the Clown suit colors) to be real. There were no seeds stuck to the inside of the lid, which looked smooth and clean.

A trail of golden wires led out of the Pumpkin Boy's head, the back part behind the eyes, nose and grinning mouth *(could there be a hidden compartment back there?)* and were bundled together with white plastic ties. There looked to be hundreds of individual hair-thin wires. The bundle ended in a curl, like a rolled hose, on the floor.

Jody saw that the Pumpkin Boy wore a pair of ordinary leather carpenter's gloves, like the ones his mother used in the garden.

Jody now realized how quiet it was.

"Hel-lo?" he said. His voice sounded like a frog's croak.

There was no answer.

Feeling stronger than he had before, Jody tried to twist himself around.

Whatever he was trussed to, it gave little, but it did give. He turned a bit to the right, then swung back, as if he were suspended on a rope. He had seen the wall beyond the Pumpkin Boy and the poster: brown, unadorned.

He twisted again, harder. His legs were asleep, which at least meant that his twisted ankle didn't hurt anymore. His hands were also asleep, but he could feel enough of them now to discover that they were tightly bound behind his back.

He tried for a time, but couldn't loosen them.

This time as he turned he saw the wall and something on the true floor: a table, a bright silver machine with a big black dial and the edge of a huge white clock face with too many numbers around the edge.

He came stubbornly back to rest.

He was growing weaker.

The Pumpkin Boy hadn't moved, was staring straight through him.

Jody gave a mighty turn, with an *ooofff!* This time he felt as if a lance had pierced his forehead. He cried out in pain, but he saw the whole silver machine, which was on casters, and other machines, one of which looked like the emergency generator Mom kept in the garage, and a door. No windows. The clown suit was draped over a single chair, next to a lamp—

The door was just opening.

Jody swung back to rest, the pain still driving through his head. He knew he was crying.

The shuffle sounded frantic.

"Ted!"

He passed out with the man's hands on his head, or what felt like through it.

A hum in his ears.

It sounded like bees, or millions of ants. He'd seen millions of ants once, two armies fighting in the forest, brown and black. He went back three days later and they were still fighting. His cousin, Jim, who was fourteen years old, told him to make a cone out of the comic book in his back pocket and when he did, and put the wide end of the cone near the massed ants and the tighter end next to his ear, he heard a roaring, a scrabble and hum that sounded like the mighty armies he saw fighting in books.

He thought Jim had played a trick on him, and took the homemade horn away from the battle, but Jim was ten feet away from him, grinning.

"Somethin', ain't it?"

"Wow."

It had sounded like this, only less so. . . .

Jody opened his eyes. It now felt like his head had been split in two like a melon. There was a dry burning behind his eyelids, and a circle of hot pain all around his head, as if a heated clamp had been tightened around it.

He heard a mewling sound, and realized it came from his mouth.

"There, Ted, there . . ."

A cool hand rested on his brow, above his eyes, and then withdrew.

The hot pain circling his head increased.

His eyes were watering, but he blinked and then could see, almost clearly. The Pumpkin Boy sat where he had been, staring mutely at nothing. To his right the silver machine with the big black dial and white clock face had been positioned at a slight angle; next to it, on another dolly, was a similar, smaller machine.

The thick bundle of hair-thin golden wires was now plugged into the side of the silver machine; another bundle was plugged into the opposite side of the machine and ran to the floor . . . toward Jody.

He cried out, in pain and terror.

"There, there, Ted . . ."

Again the soothing hand, the clown glove; as it withdrew from his face Jody saw the clown face close to his own, peering into him as if his head were a fish bowl. The lips didn't smile, nor the eyes.

"Out!"

"Yes, Ted," the soft voice sing-songed. "Yes . . ."
The clown hand came back to pat his forehead.

He writhed, tried to loosen his hands, his feet, to
snake down from his captivity.

The soothing voice became almost scolding. "Ted,
you mustn't—"

The clown hand reached out to the huge black dial
on the silver machine; Jody saw the hand grip it hard
and twist it. Pain came, and he went back to sleep.

CHAPTER TWENTY

Pictures of Jody.

She didn't know whether to take them down, put them away, turn them to the wall or put them in new frames. Nothing, Emily Wendt knew, would work. If she put them away it would be a defeat, an admission that he was gone, as well as giving up hope.

But having him staring out at her from every room in the house was almost unbearable. She had never realized how many pictures she had of her son. They were everywhere, framed on the hallway wall, in a gilt frame next to her bed, stuck under magnets on the refrigerator door, herded with other family portraits on top of the television, on the hunter's table behind the sofa, the last Sears portrait, from Christmas, on the phone table . . .

In the end, she put them all away except the one next to her bed.

That had been the first portrait she'd ever had

taken of him, when he was one. Phil had still been
alive then. She remembered how much trouble they
had keeping Jody still; the photographer had posed
him in a chair covered with a blanket and Jody, who
had recently taken his first steps, kept trying to dis-
mount it. It was obvious he was fascinated by the
camera and wanted to study it. Finally the photographer had to let him look it over, click the shutter
twice and then promise him another look if he sat
still for the picture.

You'd never know he had been any trouble by
looking at the finished product. The portrait showed
him staring quietly, with big eyes, at the camera; his
face held a measure of interest that proved he was
only thinking about getting his hands on that machine again. A lick of his thin auburn hair had fallen
over his brow (later his hair would thicken, becoming almost coarse; unless cut very short it tended
never to stay combed or brushed for long) and his
pudgy hands were folded on his lap.

This would be the picture she wouldn't put away.

Later that day, after the session, she and Jody and
Phil had gone to the taco place in the mall, the one
and only time they had ever eaten out together. She
still remembered what Jody had done to the burrito
they had gotten him, how he had dissected it like a
frog.

She found herself weeping—the first time in the
days since Jody had been taken that she had cried.
She had thought her life was over after Phil was
killed, but now she knew just how much she still
possessed, even after the loss of her husband. There

was a hollow place in her now that felt as if it had been scooped out with a trowel, and she knew it would never fill in.

This was *nothing* like it had been when Phil died.

She collapsed to the floor, hugging Jody's picture, and sat with her legs folded beneath her, rocking and crying.

"Oh, Jody. *Jody* . . ."

She thought she heard him call her name.

She froze in mid sob, and wiped her eyes with the sleeve of her sweater.

"Jody . . . ?"

She knew how foolish this was, but she *had* heard him call to her.

Forgetting the picture, she pushed herself to her feet and stumbled to the back of the house. The noise had come from the kitchen.

A blast of cold air hit her. She saw that the kitchen door leading to the backyard was open.

Holding her sweater closed, shivering, she stepped out onto the back stoop.

"Jody?" she called, almost fearfully.

The backyard was awash in unraked leaves pushed into dunes by the wind. The sky was overcast, huge banks of gray cumulus clouds rolling over one another from west to east. The temperature was falling. The pumpkin fields beyond the fence looked ominous, cold, brown and wet. The far hills surrounding Orangefield were dark, the trees stripped of green.

It looked like the landscape of a particular kind of hell.

She shivered, still holding her sweater closed, and turned around. She gasped and put her hand to her mouth.

There, staring straight up at her, was the face of a pumpkin. Puffs of steam issued from the eyes, the nose. The surface of the face looked hard and glassy, and, from within, there was a soft orange glow.

There was a body below it, the size of an older boy or young teen, sharp angles and shiny metal. The thing had its hands on her shoulders, holding her. There were gloves on its hands, but she could feel sharp metal fingers within.

The face came closer. There was a flat metallic smell, like three-in-one oil. The eyes stared into her, studying her, as if watching her from a far distance.

A long puff of metallic-smelling steam hissed forth from the mouth, which was smiling impossibly wide through its two angled teeth.

The jet of steam held a word, in the form of a question:

"Mmmmmom?" Jody said.

CHAPTER TWENTY-ONE

It was getting dark.

Len Schneider looked like a man who was thinking. He stood with his head down, hands in the pockets of his jacket.

He glanced at his watch. *Almost time to go.* His hands clenched into fists.

It had turned even colder. The last few days had each announced, with increasing earnestness, that autumn was here and winter wasn't far behind. A curt wind was whipping dead leaves into some of the shallow pits they had dug. The deeper holes were filled with muddy water and leaf blankets. There was nothing else in any of them.

Where the hell are you, you son of a bitch? His fists clenched tighter.

"Detective? We're gonna roll now."

Schneider looked up to see Fran Morrison, one of the fresh-faced uniformed cops, standing in front of him. Behind the tight cluster of trees, in a small clearing, a work crew was loading shovels and other tools into a truck—an emblem on its door, in orange letters on a black background, read TOWN OF ORANGE-FIELD, PUBLIC WORKS.

As Schneider watched, one of the crew opened the door, climbed into the truck and yanked it closed behind him.

Morrison was waiting for him to say something, so Schneider let out a long breath and said, "Yeah, Fran, we're done here. You might as well go, too."

"You need a ride back?"

Schneider looked down at his shoes, which were covered with mud. "No, I'm good."

Morrison, almost sighing with relief, turned and was gone. A few moments later Schneider heard the young cop's patrol car spitting leaves from its tires as it followed the truck down the road they had made and hooked up with a dirt road a quarter of a mile away.

He was alone now.

But he knew he wasn't. He felt it.

"Dammit!" His voice echoed through the forest.

He couldn't blame Morrison and the rest of them if they thought he was obsessed. He knew he was. But there was no way he wasn't going to do everything he could to find Jody Wendt.

And Jody Wendt was here, somewhere. Whoever had taken him had a lair here. Schneider *knew* it.

For a moment, Jerry Carlton's smirking face rose into his memory, wearing those goddamned mirror shades.

"Not this time," Schneider said out loud.

CHAPTER TWENTY-TWO

"My party this time," Grant said.

The bar itself was crowded, but the booth area, at three o'clock in the afternoon, was nearly empty. Bill Grant placed a fifth of Dewars gently on the table, as if setting down a piece of porcelain, and sat as he produced two eight ounce glasses, one with ice, one empty. He hesitated as he pushed the empty one toward Len Schneider.

"This is the way you like it, right? Neat?"

Schneider nodded. "I didn't think you were paying attention last time."

Grant gave a slight smile and pushed the empty glass to the other side of the table.

Schneider was working at the cap on the bottle, and twisted it open with practiced ease.

He poured for himself, then reached across and studied the amber liquid as it trickled over the ice in Grant's glass.

"I thought we should talk outside the office," Grant said.

Schneider's ears immediately pricked up; already he detected a focus in the man he hadn't seen before.

Len replied, still looking at the Scotch in Grant's glass, "You here to give me the fatherly pep talk? I'm sure Franny Morrison and the rest of them think I'm nuts."

He looked up from Grant's glass to meet the detective's eyes. To his surprise, Grant was smiling.

Schneider asked, "You think I'm nuts too?"

Grant's smile widened. "As a matter of fact, I do. But I understand. Thing is, I know now that this case of yours is definitely weird shit."

Schneider had downed one Scotch and refilled his own glass. Grant's new attitude had begun to irk him just as much as his old one.

"Weird enough," he said. "Did you hear what Jody Wendt's mother claims happened to her yesterday? That a pumpkin-headed robot appeared on her back stoop and spoke to her in Jody's voice?" Schneider let out a bitter laugh. "That's weird enough for me, especially when the kid vanished like a magician's rabbit."

"Frankly, I find it charming. She told me the same story."

"You interviewed her?" Schneider said with sudden anger.

"On my own time," Grant added quickly. His smile faded a bit, and he actually looked apologetic. He said, "It has nothing to do with you, Len. I just had to know."

"Had to know what?" Schneider's voice had risen—a few of the patrons at the bar, one of whom was a cop they both knew, looked at them before turning away. Schneider finished his drink and poured a third.

Grant put his hand on Schneider's arm. Schneider looked at the hand, still angry, but his anger drained when he saw that the familiar haunted look had returned to the other detective's face. Grant's skin had the yellow pallor of the cloud of smoke from his cigarette.

Schneider let a long breath out.

Grant had finished his own Scotch and was pouring a new one. He drank half of this past its ice, which had mostly melted from the natural heat of the liquor, then put the glass down. He coughed.

"Remember when I said there were worse things than a kid disappearing?"

Schneider's anger was back in an instant, but Grant immediately pushed on.

"I know how callous that sounded. Believe me, I do." He stopped for Scotch. "But I think there are things going on in Orangefield much worse than anything you can imagine."

"Like what?" Schneider replied, not hiding his mood.

"Samhain, for instance."

Schneider almost spit Scotch as he blurted a laugh. "Those kids' stories? 'Sam sightings' and all that crap? Are you kidding, Grant?"

"Never mind, then," Grant said, his voice a near whisper.

Schneider was once again reminded of the vague, haunted man in the office the day he had taken this assignment, and knew it had something to do with the Kerlan case.

Grant looked straight at Schneider, who was working on his own Scotch. "I've seen a lot of strange stuff in this town over the years, most of it around Halloween, but I never believed there was anything to it until now."

Schneider said nothing.

Grant leaned forward and said earnestly, "What do you believe in, Len? I mean, what do you *really* believe in? What would happen if something happened that made you believe not only that there might be an afterlife, but that there really was a creature that was Death itself, something you could actually fight?"

Grant's question was so unlike him, so unlike his meticulous procedural ways and evidence building, and his manner so suddenly needy, as if some sort of dam had burst within him, letting out all the fears he'd tucked away, that Schneider said nothing. He looked at his Scotch, then drank it. He started to get up.

"You know what I believe in, Bill? I believe in not fucking up a second time."

Grant grabbed his arm and urged him back into the booth. His eyes pinned Schneider in place, like a butterfly to a board. When he spoke again his voice was level and harsh. "Take me seriously, Len. The good news is that you don't have to worry about weird shit. I'll do that for both of us. The bad news is

I think you just might fuck up again, if you're not careful. I think you should let me have this case, for that reason, and because I want it. It was a mistake for you to take it to begin with. You've got that mess in Milwaukee so tied up with this that you're liable to screw up."

It was Schneider's turn to be level and harsh. He leaned forward in the booth. "That bastard Jerry Carlton sat there during his trial taking his watch apart and putting it back together. He never glanced at the jury, not once. At the end of the trial, he looked up from his watch and mouthed the word 'Ted' at me. That was the kid in Milwaukee's name." His voice was shaking. "I could have saved that kid."

"Maybe," Grant answered.

There were another two fingers of Scotch in Schneider's glass and he drained it, poured again. Tears abruptly filled his eyes. *"I could have saved him."*

"Like I said, maybe. Then again, maybe not. Maybe you still would have gotten there too late. Maybe Jerry Carlton would have killed him earlier if he saw you coming."

Schneider drained his glass and gripped it so hard that he could feel it was on the verge of breaking. He looked at Grant, who was studying him; Grant's pallor had assumed its yellow, haunted tinge.

"Be careful, Len," Grant almost whispered. "Do your job and don't let things get out of hand."

The anger was back and this time when Schneider stood up Grant didn't try to stop him.

"This case is mine, Bill. Stay the hell away from it. I don't need a goddamn mentor—especially not a burned out lush who thinks he's seen the boogeyman."

As Schnedier stalked off, Grant stared straight ahead, unconsciously pulling a cigarette from his pocket. He put it in his mouth, ready to light it as soon as he left the bar.

"Careful," he said.

CHAPTER TWENTY-THREE

Boring.

Here it was, almost time for the Pumpkin Days Festival, and Scotty Daniels was bored silly. He was sick to death of little kid stuff. In his kindergarten class, they'd already made their "special designs" for the school projects display during the festival. They had already taken their bus trip to Mr. Froelich's farm to pick their own pumpkins (although the guy they called Frankenstein, who worked for Mr. Froelich, wasn't there, darnit), and gone to the Orangefield Library to hear Ms. Marks tell ghost stories and do pumpkin cutouts for the library windows. He'd seen that creepy older kid, Annabeth Turner, staring at him from the library's second floor balcony.

They had tied yellow ribbons for Jody Wendt to one of the sycamore trees in the field behind the school, and Scotty himself, who had been one of Jody's best friends, had picked out a special pumpkin at Froelich Farm, which now sat on Jody's empty desk. There was a bulletin board in the back of the room with cards and balloons remembering Jody thumbtacked to it.

And now there was nothing to do but wait for the festival to begin.

Or . . .

Think about hunting the Pumpkin Boy.

Scotty had first heard about the hunt from his older brother Jim, but the story had traveled like wildfire through all of the schools in Orangefield. One of Jim's friends, Mitchell Freed, claimed he had seen a boy made out of silver stilts with a pumpkin head walking through one of the fields at the edge of town; Mitchell's older brother was a police officer and claimed that the Pumpkin Boy had visited Mrs. Wendt after Jody disappeared. Soon there were Pumpkin Boy sightings everywhere, so many that the *Orangefield Herald* had carried stories about it, which Jim read out loud to him.

But when he asked if he could go with Jim when he and his friends went looking for the Pumpkin Boy tonight, Jim had only laughed and ruffled his hair.

"No, way, little man! Mom would kill me if I took you." He looked suddenly serious and said, "And anyway, Mitch and Paul and I might get killed!"

Then he laughed and walked away to use the phone.

Scotty could hear him using it now, arranging for

Mitchell to come by in ten minutes and that they'd go in Jim's car.

Bored.

Scotty wandered into the family room, where his younger sister Cyndi was watching the Cartoon Network. He sat down grumpily next to her on the couch and tried to wrestle the TV remote from her hands. She clutched it tightly and said, "Hey!" Finally he gave up and threw himself onto the far end of the couch among the sofa pillows and folded his arms, feeling ornery.

He glanced out the window to the street, where a passing car's headlights momentarily blinded him. He continued staring, and when his sight came back he was staring at Jim's car at the curb.

The trunk was open.

A sudden idea formed in his mind.

At that moment he heard Jim get off the phone, yell down to the basement to tell his father that he'd be going out for a little while. After his father answered with a grunt, he heard Jim, loudly as always, go into the bathroom in the hallway, slamming the door behind him. In a moment there was water running, and the sound of Jim's bad singing voice.

Scotty got up off the couch and walked past Cyndi, who didn't even look his way, her eyes glued to the television screen.

Scotty went quickly to the hallway, removed his jacket from its hook and put it on. He eased open the front door and slipped out, closing the door with a quiet *click* behind him.

It was chilly out, and there was a breeze. Scotty zipped his jacket all the way up to his chin and ran to Jim's car.

The trunk was indeed open. Inside were the bundled old newspapers that Jim was supposed to bring to the recycling center. There were three bundles, thrown in carelessly.

Scotty pushed two of them aside, snugged himself into the trunk, and then worked the trunk lid partway down.

He hesitated. From around the corner, someone appeared, walking briskly. It was Jim's friend, Mitch.

Scotty held his breath and snuggled down. Whistling, Mitch bounded past the car and up the steps to the front door of the house. Scotty peeked out. At that moment the front door opened, swallowing Mitch. Without further hesitation, Scotty closed the trunk all the way.

He heard the solid *click* of the latch, but immediately saw the glowing escape bar that Jim had showed him when he'd bought the new car. Of course Jim had showed him how it worked—then told him a few gruesome stories about older cars that didn't have the device, and what had happened to the kids who had been trapped inside. One of them, which Scotty didn't believe, involved a baby that had accidently been locked in the trunk of a car one summer day in 1960: "And when they opened the trunk that night they found the baby cooked alive, looking just like a roasted pig!"

Scotty began to think about that baby. His heart

pounded, and he was just about to reach for the glow bar and sneak back into the house when he heard the front door of the house open. Almost immediately, the car rocked on its shocks as Jim and Mitch jumped into it.

In another second the car pulled away from the curb, the two older boys laughing.

Almost immediately, they started to talk about girls.

They made one other stop, and Scotty heard one other boy, who he guessed was Paul Henry, get into the car. The talk was still about girls, but then it eventually turned to the Pumpkin Boy.

"You think he's real?" Paul Henry's voice asked.

Mitch immediately answered, "It's real, man. I told you what my brother said. It's a fact that it went to Jody Wendt's house, scared his old lady half crazy. Dragged her into the house after she fainted, then left. And my brother said a couple of tourists from Montreal were picking pumpkins out at Kranepool's Farm and saw it walking through the woods. Just taking a stroll. My brother talked to them himself. He says there are at least ten other reports on file. One guy said he threw rocks at it, but he was drunk, so the cops didn't take him too seriously. The Pumpkin Boy's real, all right."

"What if we really find it?" Jim said. There was uncertainty in his voice.

"If we find it, we kill it!" Paul Henry said. "Then we get the reward money!"

"There isn't any reward money," Mitch replied immediately. "Use your head, Paul! If we bring it in in one piece, we'll get in the papers. Then maybe somebody will write a book, and we'd be in that, too. If there's a book we could probably get some money out of it."

"I still say knock it to pieces!" Paul answered. "I ain't letting that thing near me!"

"You bring the camera, Paul?" Jim asked idly.

There was silence for a moment, then Paul Henry's dejected voice mumbled, "I forgot."

Jim and Mitch roared with laughter.

Jim said, "That's okay, Paul. I brought my kid brother's camera. You're covered. Here, take it. And don't lose it."

Scotty almost shouted out with annoyance, but kept his tongue.

"Good," Paul said. "If we get a picture, that would be almost as good as capturing him. I bet the *Herald* would pay us for that."

Mitch laughed. "I heard they've already gotten a bunch of phoney pictures. One of them was a scarecrow with a pumpkin for a head."

Jim chimed in. "There was a story in the paper today. Another photo they got was of some guy's kid with a costume on, holding a pumpkin in front of his face!"

They all laughed. In the trunk, Scotty smiled. Jim had read him that story.

Suddenly the car moved from smooth road to a bumpier surface. It was harder to hear what the boys were saying with the added noise. One of them—it sounded like Paul—said, "How much farther?"

"Couple miles," Jim answered. "I want to get as

close to the site as we can. You sure the police won't bother us, Mitch?"

"My brother said they packed up and moved out. Dug a bunch of holes but found nothing."

"You really think this Pumpkin Boy snatched Jody Wendt?"

Mitch replied, "Who knows? Most of the places he's been seen are around this spot. You got a better idea?"

Again there was silence.

"I still say we should kill him," Paul Henry said.

"Maybe he'll kill *you!*" Jim said, and then there was another, longer, silence.

Eventually the car came to a stop after hitting a pothole.

"I think we ought to leave it here," Jim said, his voice clearer.

"Sounds good to me," Mitch said.

Car doors opened and then closed. There were sounds of fumbling and then Scotty heard them leaving the car.

The shuffling footsteps suddenly stopped.

"Hey, Paul, did you bring the camera?"

Amidst more laughter, Paul said, "Shit," and Scotty heard a car door open and then close again.

"Yeah, I've got it."

"And you brought a flashlight?"

Again the word: "*Shit!*"

Mitch laughed. "Stay with me, bozo. If we find the Pumpkin Boy, we'll let him eat you."

"Eat *this*," came Paul Henry's reply, and again there was laughter.

The voices, laughter and shuffling steps receded.

In a few moments, Scotty was alone. And suddenly, he *felt* alone. He realized he had not brought a flashlight, either.

And where was he going to go? He had no idea where he was, or where to look. He knew his only chance to find the Pumpkin Boy was to trail along after his brother and his two friends. Otherwise, he might as well stay in the trunk of the car.

He reached out and pushed the glow bar. Instantly, the trunk popped open. Scotty climbed out.

It was not as dark as he feared. There was a fat rising moon, which peeked through the trees with yellow-gray light, and Scotty's eyes were already used to being in the dark from being in the car trunk. The car was parked on the side of a rutted dirt road with thick woods to either side.

He could still hear Jim and his friends, though barely; there was a blurt of laughter and he went that way, to the left of the car, into the woods.

To his relief, there was a narrow path, half-covered in leaves and pine needles.

The laughter came again, a little closer, but still far away. And then, suddenly, there was real silence. It was as if a stifling cloak had been thrown over the forest—nothing moved or breathed.

Scotty became very afraid, to the point where he had no further interest in the Pumpkin Boy. All he wanted to do was go back to the car and wait for his brother to come back.

He turned around, but now was unsure which way he had come. The path had branched off and there were two paths in front of him, split into a fork. He walked tentatively up one, looking for the scuff marks of his own sneakers, but it was smooth and untouched.

He turned back to find the other path, but now couldn't locate it.

The moon dipped into clouds, leaving darkness, then burst out with orange light like the light through venetian blinds, cut into slats.

Scotty had no idea where he was.

He heard a single sound, a loud *thump*, and then stifling silence again, as if the forest were waiting.

Then, a faraway snort of laughter.

He wanted to head in that direction, but there was no path.

Then he saw a flash of light, close by.

"Jim?" he called out, loudly.

The light flashed again, just ahead and to the left of the path he was on. He walked in that direction. A third glint, and he broke through a rank of bushes and found himself in a clearing.

The moon glared down, higher now, filling the leaf-scattered bare spot he was in with orange-gray light. He took a step and fell into a depression filled with leaves. He sank almost to his knees, then waded to the lip and pulled himself out.

Now he saw that he was surrounded by holes and depressions. It was like being on the cratered moon. He remembered what his brother and Mitch had talked about in the car: a place where the police had been, full of holes.

Now he became very afraid.

There were muted sounds all around him now: rustlings, the break of a twig, scampering sounds. He felt like he was going to wet himself, and closed his eyes, begining to whimper.

A rasping voice said: "Scccotty?"

He thought he knew the voice, and opened his eyes with hope—

But it wasn't Jim.

Scotty yelped.

The Pumpkin Boy stood right in front of him, his huge orange jack o'-lantern head glinting in the sallow moonlight.

"Ohhh . . ." Scotty wet himself.

The Pumpkin Boy cocked his head to one side; his smile, lit dimly from within, looked almost comical. When he spoke again a slight hiss of steam issued from his mouth and eyes and nose holes: "Sccccotty, it's me. Jody Wennnndt."

A portion of Scotty's fear left him, but he was still trembling. The wet spot on the front of his jeans and down one leg began to feel cold.

With a series of little creaks, the Pumpkin Boy sat down on the leaves in front of Scotty. His thin metal limbs jutted out in all directions. "Sit down, Scccotty. Talk to mmme."

Scotty felt himself almost collapse to sit in front of the mechanical man.

"Is . . . it really . . . you?" Scotty got out in a halting whisper.

"I . . . thinnnk so. I can see, and wwwwalk, and talk. It feels like I'm in a ddddream. And my hhh-head hurts all the ttttime."

144

"I . . ." Scotty didn't know what to say.

"And I nnnnever sleep now. And my eyes are hhh-hot."

"You went to your house . . . ?"

"Yes, I ccccan't do that again. He won't llllet me. He ccccontrols what I do."

"Who?"

As if he had forgotten something, the Pumpkin Boy suddenly unfolded his limbs and stood up. The process seemed to take a long time. There was the faint odor of machine oil and heated air.

Scotty looked up; the Pumpkin Boy was now looming over him, his gloved hands opening and closing.

"I'm ssssorry, Sccccotty," Jody whispered.

"For what?" Scotty said.

With the sound of metal sliding on metal, and a faint metallic groan, the Pumpkin Boy reached down and gripped Scotty around his waist. Scotty felt himself hoisted up and then pressed tight to the Pumpkin Boy's cylindrical chest.

He heard a faint beating there.

The smell of oil was stronger.

The Pumpkin Boy walked, with Scotty pressed tight against him with one enfolding arm.

Scotty, his own heart hammering, counted five long steps.

He let out a long weak cry.

Jody's voice said, very softly, "I'm ssssorry, Sccc-cotty, but he says I'm not a ggggood Ted."

CHAPTER TWENTY-FOUR

Grant felt as yellow and dried out as he knew he looked. It was getting bad again, like it always did before Pumpkin Days began. He couldn't get through the mornings without that first drink at breakfast, and, by lunch, if he didn't already have a pint in him, his hands began to shake and he couldn't concentrate.

But, with the booze in him, he was as good at his job as he ever was.

He still knew he was a great cop—even if he was a walking car wreck. And today, with the first pint already smoothly settled in his gut and veins, he could even face the coming Pumpkin Days Festival itself.

God, how he hated this town—and loved it. As Len Schneider had told him, people were the same all over, a healthy cocktail of good and rotten, and they were no better or worse here in Orangefield. There was greed, corruption, untamed anger, cheating, thievery and, occasionally, even murder, just like anywhere else on the good ol' Earth. All the deadly sins, all in a pretty row. But Orangefield was one of the lucky communities of the rotten creatures called men that had learned to put a good face on it. They had dolled it up, made it pretty, which, somehow, made it bearable. The entire history of Orangefield was one long cavalcade of greed, one long pursuit of money, and the town fathers had finally, when they discovered—and then exploited—the serendipitous fact that pumpkins grew here like nowhere else on the planet, found a way to have their cake and eat it too. They could make money hand over fist, and, like Las Vegas, still pretend to be one of those "nice" places to live. Good schools, good facilities, good services, a mayor who always smiled and a police force who kept things in order.

As corrupt and rotten as anywhere else, only with a much better makeup job.

Grant took a deep breath, coughed and chided himself; he knew damn well how cynical he had become, and knew that many of his problems came from something outside the normal proclivities of Orangefield itself.

From, for instance, the fact that he now believed not only that Samhain existed, but that he didn't want Grant anywhere near whatever weird shit he was up to.

"Stay out of it. . . ."

Which was something, of course, that Grant could not do.

He shivered, a physical reaction, and ducked off the empty midway of the main festival tent into an empty space behind one of the booths. He could hear the sound of hammers as workmen erected tables and stages behind him. He fumbled the new pint out of his raincoat pocket and twisted the top off with shaking fingers, putting the bottle quickly to his lips.

Two long gulps, another racking cough and some of the demons went away.

This would be a bad day, and he would end up in his bed alone tonight, his wife once again in Killborne, the institution, and he would awake with the night sweats, and insomnia and a hangover with all its own requisite horrors. . . .

Still, he felt like he had a job to do.

One that Len Schneider wasn't doing.

He screwed the cap firmly back onto the bottle and thrust it deep into his pocket.

No more until you're finished for the day, Billy boy. He took a deep breath. *You're still a cop. The best.*

He looked at his trembling hand, which eventually steadied under his willful gaze.

Go to work.

Grant was in the midway again, standing out in the lights under the huge tent, with the ebb and flow of the workmen around him. It was like being at a carnival, only one dominated by a single color: everything, *everything*, was in shades of orange. The tent was orange and white-striped, the booths hung with orange crepe paper, the display tables covered with orange tablecloths. Light was provided by hanging lanterns shaped like pumpkins.

And everything soon to be displayed would be pumpkin related. There would be pumpkin toys, forty different foods made from pumpkins, books on pumpkins, school projects made from pumpkins, the biggest pumpkin, the smallest pumpkin . . .

Music drifted in from outside the main tent— there was a bandstand in the auxiliary tent, and tonight was practice night for forties dance music. He did not want to be here when it was rap night.

The lights overhead flickered and there was a gust of chilled October air, so different from the summer-like warmth of only a couple of weeks ago. . . .

He was entering what would be the entertainment section of the midway: nickel and dime games of chance (proceeds to charity), a local magician, a balloon toy maker who was practicing his craft. The hiss of helium brought an oddly nostalgic tinge to Grant's mind: he remembered when television was in black and white and on Saturday morning there was a guy who twisted impossibly long balloons, which he first inflated with that same insistent hiss, into impossibly intricate animals—a giraffe, a rabbit, a dachshund. He paused for a moment at the booth—this guy was not as good. His latest creation was something that looked like a duck, but which the balloon-twister proclaimed an eagle.

Grant stifled a laugh and moved on to other booths and displays: someone was practicing his spiel selling rug shampoo, and had managed to procure a bright orange rug to demonstrate on; a pumpkin cookie stand; a pumpkin-colored pretzel stand; a dark, long, well-enclosed booth with flaps over the cutout windows—inside there were rows of benches in the dark, and an ancient 16mm movie projector would show black-and-white cartoons against the back wall. Grant peeked in. Dark and empty.

He turned away—another reflection from his own childhood, only he wondered how many kids, in the era of video games and computers and digital television, would sit still for a grainy old Betty Boop film.

A wide, high booth near the end of the midway caught Grant's eye. Immediately, and for no reason he could put his finger on, that sixth sense that he knew made him a good cop tickled and came alive.

There was something about it, about the guy who was in it pacing around alone. . . .

The booth was brightly lit, deep and wide. Behind a rope barrier covered with crinkly black and orange crepe paper, on a white wooden platform far away so that he couldn't be touched, a clown solemnly practiced. He was dressed in orange and black motley, his head topped with a white hat with an orange pom, his face painted white with a huge orange smile and black lashes completely circling his eyes. He was juggling three balls, two orange, one white.

Behind him, plastered on the back of the wall, was a huge, grotesque poster of a more vivacious clown dressed in brighter clothing, which proclaimed, UNCLE LOLLIPOP LOVES YOU! On the bottom of the poster, in small letters, was written: BROUGHT TO YOU FROM MADISON, WISCONSIN.

The little tickle of awareness in Grant's head turned to a buzz of recognition.

Wisconsin . . .

My God, maybe this has nothing to do with Samhain at all.

Could this be Jerry Carlton?

Grant studied the clown for a moment: he was of medium height, medium weight. His lips were thin inside the painted smile. His eyes were empty, staring at nothing.

Grant's first instinct was to reach for his service revolver, but then the immediate thought struck him that if this was Carlton, then those two boys would be close by.

Grant quickly moved past the remaining booths—an orange juice stand, a table selling gardening tools—MAKE YOUR PUMPKINS THE BIGGEST IN ORANGE-FIELD! a homemade sign proclaimed—and pushed through the tent flap to the outside.

Crisp night air assaulted him. The band music, "Don't Sit Under the Apple Tree," not played very well, was louder. Rainier Park was filled with strollers and curiosity seekers impatient for the Pumpkin Festival to begin, a lot of teenagers milling in groups, the occasional policeman put on extra duty since the second child abduction.

He hurriedly lit a cigarette.

Butt firmly between his lips, Grant buttoned his raincoat as he walked around the tent to the back facing the booths he had just observed.

A cloud darker than the night sky came toward him, and he held his breath as it resolved into what looked like a swarm of hornets.

He waited for a voice, but none came.

The cloud fell to the ground and swirled past him: a tornado of tiny leaves moved by the wind.

There were vehicles parked in a ragged line— Winnebagos, SUVs, a couple of old station wagons, at the far end a semi with BIFFORD FOODS painted on the truck in bold letters. Grant counted down from his end to approximate the back location of the clown's booth, and found a large white panel truck without markings bearing Wisconsin rental plates.

The hair on the back of his neck stood up.

He studied the back of the truck: there were two outwardly hinged doors, closed at the middle and locked through a hasp and staple with a large, heavy, new-looking padlock. The front of the truck was empty, the door locked, no key in the ignition.

He walked to the back and put his hand on one of the doors.

In a fierce whisper, he called out: "Jody? Scott?"

There was no answer.

He slapped on the door with the flat of his hand, and put his ear to it, but was met with only silence.

What he wanted to do and what he was supposed to do were two different things. He wanted to borrow the nearest crowbar and pry open the back of the panel truck. But if he did that, no matter what he found, none of it would be admissible in a court of law.

Even "just cause" wouldn't cover it.

Then again, if he did nothing, he would not be able to live with himself for much longer. If that truck held what he feared it held and he did nothing, and his hesitation was the difference between those two boys being alive and dead, he knew that the demon memories that chased him, the things he wouldn't *think* about, never mind talk about, would catch up, and that would be the end of him.

He thought of Len Schneider briefly—this was, in essence, Schneider's dilemma: *I waited too long. . . .*

Grant tramped farther down the line of vehicles, avoiding thick electrical lines that led from the tent to ground outlets farther off, till he came upon two men sitting on the dropped back end of a pickup truck and smoking. He showed them his badge, angling it in the faint light so they could see it.

"You guys have a crowbar?"

One of the smokers flicked his cigarette away and nodded. "Sure thing."

In a moment Grant had what he needed. Gripping the strong metal bar, he went back to the panel truck.

Throwing his own cigarette aside, he angled the crowbar into the curl of the lock's closure and gave a single hard yank.

With a weak groan, the lock snapped open and fell away with a *clank*.

One of the doors, uneven on its hinges, swung slowly toward Grant, opening.

Light filtered into the back of the truck, illuminating the interior.

"Shit almighty," Grant whispered.

CHAPTER TWENTY-FIVE

Len Schneider dreamed. Except for the one about the kid with no face, he rarely dreamt. But when he did they were significant.

In this one, he was flying like a bird. He had wings with long blue feathers, white-tipped, and he soared high into the clouds and then dived, his mouth open in exultation.

And then, in the manner of dreams, things changed, and he was in a balloon. His wings were gone. He was floating, at the mercy of the wind. The basket, which was constructed in a loose weave that let him see through the breaks in the bottom, shifted precariously when he moved, threatening to break apart. But he was unafraid, and held tightly to the ropes, which secured the gondola to the balloon. He peered calmly out.

He was passing over a huge green forest, which spread out below him in all directions. At one horizon was a line of mountains, impossibly tall and thin, their peaks like snow-capped needles. The sun was either setting or rising. A glint of something that might have been a vast body of water shimmered in the direction opposite the sun.

But he studied the trees.

Suddenly (as is the manner in dreams), he held a spyglass in one hand. He peered through it, and the tops of the trees looked close enough to touch. While still looking through the glass he reached down and *did* touch the tops of trees, feeling the light brush of healthy leaves vaguely redolent of moisture against his fingers.

And then something rose large as a whale into his vision, and he felt the flat, hard touch of an artificial structure slide under his hand.

When he stood up gasping, and threw the spyglass away, the thing had already disappeared behind him. When he looked back anxiously he saw nothing but the receding tops of trees waving their leaves at him, going away—

"Jesus!"

Schneider opened his eyes. For a moment he was still in the dream, which he needed no interpretation for: he could smell the rushing high air from the gondola and the faint hot breath of the balloon overhead; he moved his arms and for the briefest second thought they were ridged with feathers.

"*Jesus,*" he gasped, fully awake now, and jumped out of bed and began to dress quickly, strapping on his shoulder holster.

CHAPTER TWENTY-SIX

"That's right: Carlton. C-A-R-L-T-O-N," Grant said. The voice on the other end of the line said some words, and then Grant answered: "No, the panel truck was empty, but I still think he's the guy who took the kids. Call it a gut feeling." More words from the other end, and then Grant once more: "That's right, he was gone when I went back into the tent."

The phone receiver pressed tight to his ear, Grant tried to shake another cigarette out of the pack, but found it was empty. Grunting in displeasure, he crumpled the pack with his free hand and fumbled in his raincoat for another. He coughed. His hand found the pint bottle but moved impatiently past it. Amongst loose change he located the new pack and grunted again, this time in pleasure, as he drew it out and expertly opened it, tapping a butt out and lighting it.

While he waited on the phone he turned to regard Deputy Sheriff Charlie Fredericks, who he had grabbed from his post at the entrance to the music tent in Ranier Park and brought to the station with him. The kid was bright and willing, and hadn't opened his mouth about this not being sheriff's business. Charlie was young, but he had seen his own share of weird shit in Orangefield.

Grant said to him, "Anything on who rented that panel truck?"

A second receiver pressed to his own ear, Charlie made a face. "On hold."

"Dammit. You tell them this is an emergency?"

Charlie looked hurt, then gave a sour grin. "Guess that's why they didn't just hang up."

Grant scowled, then pressed his receiver tighter to his ear. "Yes? You sure?" There was a pause. "Well, thanks, Warden."

He hung up the phone and traded puzzled looks with Charlie Fredericks, who was still on hold.

"Jerry Carlton is safe in his cell at Madison State Prison, reading an old copy of *National Geographic* as we speak," Grant said.

"Maybe an accomplice?" Charlie asked, trying to be helpful. "Someone he worked with who didn't get caught?"

"Carlton killed five boys, all on his own. He was a loner." He gave a heavy sigh. "I've got to talk to Len Schneider, find out if there was someone else. . . ."

Charlie nodded absently, giving sudden interest to his own phone. Grant suspended his own punch-dialing expectantly.

Charlie said, "Shit," and looked at Grant. "They just changed the music, is all."

Grant shook his head and jabbed in Schneider's number.

It rang until the answering machine took it.

"Isn't Schneider off tonight?" Grant said to no one in particular.

Charlie Fredericks shrugged, then said, "Yes?" into his receiver and began to nod. His pencil went to work on his notepad.

Behind Bill Grant the voice of Chip Prohman, the night sergeant, fat and laconic and nearly useless, chimed in. "You looking for Schneider? He called in a little while ago. I just sent two black-and-whites out after him. He sounded out of his head—claimed those two kidnapped kids were out in the woods after all."

Grant was about to answer when Charlie Fredericks hung up and waved his notepad at him. Grant squinted forward to read what it said.

"Holy God." Grant turned viciously on Prohman and spat, "Where the hell is Schneider?"

The sergeant answered, "Out in the woods—"

"*Where?*"

Prohman was almost yawning. "Same spot he dug all those holes. You ask me, he's just plain off his—"

Grant was already half out the door, with Charlie Fredericks, perplexed, studying the name on his notepad as if it were an ancient rune telling him nothing, behind him.

CHAPTER TWENTY-SEVEN

Grant could see the roof flashers of the cruisers ahead of him. He felt as if he were in a dream. Charlie Fredericks had talked all the tire-screaming way out, but Grant felt as if he were alone in the car.

It all came down to this.

To this—the most horrible thing of all—at least in this world.

For a tiny moment he almost wished it was the other business, weird shit, that he was dealing with. With a shiver, he let that thought go.

His only hope was that he wasn't too late.

The car bumped in and out of two successive dirt ruts, and he slammed the brakes as he pulled up behind the first of the lined-up patrol cars.

There wasn't a cop in sight, but flashlight beams danced in the woods off to the left.

His gun was already out of its holster as he pushed himself out of the car.

"Hey, Bill!" Charlie Fredericks shouted behind him, unheard.

Grant pushed through the brush as if it wasn't there; dried vines and branches slapped at his arms and across his face.

Behind him, Charlie, his own flashlight on, made his way carefully along the path into the woods.

Grant heard voices now, one of them loud and irrational:

"Hold those lights on the front of it, dammit!"

Grant broke into the clearing, into a tableau from a nightmare.

Like a nightmare, there was a strangely ethereal beauty to it. Three uniformed police officers stood stock still, holding their flashlight beams on a single spot up in the trees. The gnarled mass of denuded branches at first showed nothing to the eye, they were so tangled and uniform—and then the eye resolved a section of them pinpointed by the triple beams into a man-made opening, a brown door set neatly into the branches.

In the doorway, frozen in place and looking confused and lost, staring straight into the lights pinning him like a butterfly, was the orange and white motleyed clown Grant had seen in the tent at Ranier Park. His pom-pomed cap was gone, showing a thinning head of light-colored hair; there were rips in his orange and black costume and his makeup was smeared, pulling his smile into a high, grotesque grin on one side. The blacking around his eyes that had been used to line his lashes had run together.

On the ground in front of the three police officers, Len Schneider, looking disheveled himself, a pajama top peeking between his shirt and pants, stood in a two-handed firing position, his eye sighting down the barrel of his .38 police special, trained tightly on the figure in the doorway.

Grant, holding his own revolver at his side in a tight grip, said, in as reasonable a voice as he could, "Len, put your gun down. It's all right. He's Ted Marigold's father, Lawrence Marigold."

There were tears streaming down Schneider's face, but his hands were rock steady on his revolver. "He's Jerry Carlton!" he screamed. "And this time I got here in time!"

Grant kept his voice level, but slowly brought his handgun up. "Jerry Carlton is in Madison State Prison, Len. I talked to the warden there twenty minutes ago. The man you're aiming at is Lawrence Marigold, the father of the last kid Carlton killed. Ted's father. Remember him, Len? The genius robotics engineer? How he went insane after his son was murdered? He escaped from his institution. You couldn't save Ted, but you can save Ted's father. Just lower your gun."

Schneider ignored Grant. *"I told you!"* he screeched at the figure in the doorway. *"Send them down now!"*

The clown turned away for a moment, and then a long rope ladder rolled out of the doorway like a red carpet, its end swinging to rest just inches from the ground. The clown stepped aside, and Jody Wendt appeared in the doorway and carefully descended the ladder.

"Jesus," said Charlie Fredericks, who had stopped beside Grant and was aiming his own flashlight at the opening.

"Now the other one!" Schneider screamed.

The clown moved aside and said something that sounded like a sob. "Ted."

There was darkness in the doorway and then something else, not a boy but boy-sized, with impossibly thin, bright metal limbs and a head made of a pumpkin. It climbed out and began to descend the ladder with practiced ease. Little puffs of steam issued from the cutout holes in its face as it came down, gazing mechanically back and forth.

Charlie gasped and said: *"Je-sus!"*

Grant's own gun hand began to tremble, but he steadied it with the realization that what he was looking at was something real, something that had been made by a man.

The Pumpkin Boy stood at the bottom of the tree, next to Jody Wendt. He continued to stare back and forth, with a look almost of fright on his cartoon face. His gaze finally settled on Jody. "I'm sssssscared . . . ," he said in a horribly distorted, faraway voice.

"Where's the other boy! Where's Scotty Daniels!" Len Schneider screamed, his attention still riveted on the doorway in the trees.

"I . . . ," the clown said confusedly, his voice swallowed by the night. Then he turned back into the doorway and disappeared.

Grant took the opportunity to say, "Len, please listen—"

"Shut up! Shut the hell up!" Schneider wheeled on him for a moment with the gun, his eyes wild. Grant could see the muscles standing out like taut cables in his neck. "If you shoot me in the leg, Grant, to try to stop me, I'll blow the bastard's head off!"

There was movement in the treehouse doorway and with an almost animal growl Schneider swung his aim back that way.

"Here," the clown said.

Charlie Fredericks gave a shout of horror: there in the doorway was the body of a young boy, trussed upside down and suspended from some sort of wheeled rack. On his head was a silver cap with a thick arm of wires leading from it.

"Oh, God, what did he do to that poor kid," Charlie Fredericks said, reaching for his own revolver.

Even Grant hesitated, starting to move the aim of his gun from Len Schneider to the doorway of the treehouse. "Son of a . . ."

The boy moved. He twitched in his bonds, looking like Houdini trying to make an escape.

"Let him go, Carlton! Now!"

Lawrence Marigold made a confused motion, and then his shoulders sagged. He looked down at the pumpkin-headed robot at the bottom of the rope ladder, who turned his face up to regard him.

Marigold sobbed out, "Do you remember . . . what I used to say to you when you were a baby, Ted? When it was just you and me and Mommy, and I stopped at the store after work and bought you the candy you loved? Do you remember what I always said after you squealed and held your hands out, laughing, when I gave you your candy? *Do you remember what I used to say? Uncle Lollipop loves you!"*

Still weeping, he disappeared into the opening, then reappeared, reached down and did something to the bundle of wires on the boy's metal skullcap.

And then something happened that caused even Len Schneider to open his mouth in wonder.

The steam issuing from the Pumpkin Boy's facial cutouts increased in intensity until an orange fog engulfed its head. A thin trail of something that resembled fire and smelled like ozone curled out of the cloud, rose up the bole of the tree and snaked into the treehouse opening.

Two flashes of lightning lit up the doorway. Grant could see the edge of another poster inside the hut like the one the clown had mounted in the tent in Rainier Park.

The boy suspended from the rack began to writhe and cry out in pain.

On the ground, the Pumpkin Boy stood mute.

Len Schneider again had his .38 trained on the treehouse doorway. *"Cut him down! Now!"*

In another few moments the boy was loose and rubbing his hands and legs.

Lawrence Marigold, his face a nightmare of streaked makeup and tears, stood dumbly as Scotty Daniels climbed slowly down the ladder.

"Get the kids out of here, Charlie," Grant said. "And if anything happens to me, I want you to do me a favor. I want you to follow up on any weird shit that happens this Halloween."

"I don't get you, Bill."

"Anything weird at all. Sam sightings, anything out of the ordinary. You promise?"

"Sure, Bill. Even though—"

"Just do it. Now get those kids away."

Fredericks nodded. When Scotty reached the ground he herded the two young boys, Jody Wendt limping slightly, away from the Pumpkin Boy and down the path to the cars.

Grant thought, *At least they won't see any of this.* Out loud he said, "Len, you've got to put the gun down right now. It's all over. You did a great job."

"I won't make any mistakes this time, Carlton!" Schneider screamed, ignoring him.

"I just borrowed them!" Lawrence Marigold said, throwing his arms out in supplication. "I thought you would let me!"

Grant saw Schneider straighten his aim. *"Not this time, Carlton!"*

Oh, God, Grant thought, his own finger tightening on the trigger of his police special. In the next second split second he thought, *Goddammit, Len, don't make me do it—*

Two shots that sounded like the echo of one rang out.

Two bodies crumpled.

Shit!

Grant saw that, by the length of the time he had allowed himself to think, he had been too late to save Lawrence Marigold.

Len Schneider was down, unmoving, and in the doorway of the tree hut Marigold collapsed with a huffing grunt. He sat tilted on the sill of the tree hut for a moment, then fell forward.

He hit the ground a moment later, groaned once and was silent.

Grant walked over and knelt down to study his face.

It had the same lost, mad look it must have held for many months and years, since the night his boy had been taken.

"I'm so sorry," Grant said.

"Ted . . . ," the clown whispered, staring past Grant at nothing, and then was silent forever.

Grant stood up. Two of the uniforms were working on Len Schneider, but Grant knew it was a waste of time. He hadn't missed. He was good at his job.

Hands shaking, he lit a cigarette, coughed and thought about the bottle he would have to open later.

And Jerry Carlton sat snug and warm, reading a magazine in his cell at Madison State Prison.

Idly, Grant wondered if the warden would let him visit with Carlton, just for those three minutes Len Schneider had so badly wanted.

CHAPTER TWENTY-EIGHT

"I didn't expect to be back here so soon," Grant said.

"Neither did I." District Attorney Morton kept his hands folded before him. There was no coroner this time, no beekeeper, only the DA and Grant facing each other across a flat marble-topped table, which was cool to the touch.

Like my career, Grant thought.

"You know why you were suspended," Morton said. Grant noticed that he was not making eye contact.

"Of course."

"Thing is, Captain Farrow and I thought it would be best if you went away for a while. I understand your wife is in Killborne, and that you don't have any children, so I . . . suppose you wouldn't have much in the way of arrangements to make. We'd like you to leave today."

Grant's eyes widened, and Morton must have

caught it out of the corner of his eye, because he continued, almost in a rush. "The thing is, with this . . . friendly fire shooting coming so close on the heels of that Kerlan business—"

"It wasn't a friendly fire shooting. Len Schneider was going to shoot Lawrence Marigold, and I shot Schneider to prevent that."

"Which you didn't."

Grant looked down at the table, lips tight. "No."

Morton seemed to take strength from Grant's momentary lack of strength. Now he was making eye contact, and his eyes were suddenly hard.

"We're treating it as friendly fire, for the good of everyone involved," he said. His voice became harder. "Including you. There's a place in Phoenix, Arizona, which the Mayor and I frequent. Warm as toast this time of year. Golf course and pool, casino gambling. You can come back just before Thanksgiving, reinstated at full pay."

"Do I have a choice?" Now Grant's own voice was hard, and he was locking stares with the DA.

"No," Morton said, then he looked away. "If you . . . don't agree to this, the only other choice is immediate dismissal, an official inquiry and possible manslaughter charges. I can guarantee the first two. You realize your . . . drinking problem and your wife, Rose's . . . own problems will inevitably come up during any inquiry or trial."

"I get it," Grant said. He suddenly got up, still tight lipped, and, to his surprise, Morton rose, too.

"There'll be someone from this office out there to keep you compnay."

"A minder."

Morton nodded. "If you try to come back, the deal's off. And you'll be arrested in Arizona, then extradited." He took a long breath. "It's best for everybody, Bill," he said, putting out his fleshy hand.

Grant did not take the hand, but kept his eyes on the DA. "Especially you and the mayor," he said. His eyes suddenly narrowed. "Or is there someone else behind this?"

"Who else would there be?" Morton said, his expression showing puzzlement.

Grant held his gaze for a moment, then he shook his head and turned to leave. "See you in a month."

Morton watched the empty doorway, and then sat down heavily in his chair. He drew his extended hand back, and now it began to shake. He snatched a large white handkerchief from his breast pocket and dabbed at his forehead with it.

You did fine, the voice in his ear said.

"Who are you?" Morton asked in a whisper.

Someone who keeps his promises. And I promise to leave you alone—for now.

"For now?"

He was met with sudden silence.

•

PART III

THREE WILL SHOW THE WAY

CHAPTER TWENTY-NINE

Call me Sam.

Kathy Marks heard the voice like a cold finger drawn down the inside of her skull. It didn't sound like a voice at all. And it seemed to tickle at the darkest reaches of her memory. . . .

She looked up from the front desk of the Orange-field Library and glanced at the nearest window, which was half covered in a paper pumpkin cutout, crayon-colored side facing outward. Even though the holiday was a week away, they'd had the annual Halloween drawing contest for the four- to eight-year-olds that afternoon, which had culminated in a frenzy of scissor snipping followed by the scotch tape mounting of the winners in the front windows. A week ago, during the awful Jody Wendt business, she'd hosted a Halloween party in the library for the boy's class, and they had also taped paper cutouts to the windows.

There was no one at the window now—only the faintest whisper of a chill wind outside brushing the pane and making it moan.

Idly, Kathy scratched her left arm, gently soothing the ghostly itch of an old scar.

As if on cue, the streetlights outside the library winked on, turning autumn twilight bright again. Kathy Marks jumped involuntarily, then laughed lightly, shaking her head.

She turned back to the paperwork on her desk.

The library was closed; the front door had been locked for twenty minutes. Her assistants, Marjorie and Paul, high school students earning extra credit, had gone home. Soon she would leave for her own home, but there was no hurry.

There never was: she was thirty-two years old and alone. Almost a cliché, the spinster librarian. She had always had the feeling, ever since she was young, that she was waiting for something.

Waiting for something coming . . .

Librarian. Open the door.

There it was again—a wind that sounded like a voice.

This time Kathy looked at the offending window with the same stern stare she used on talkers in the library.

Don't do it, she told herself, *because I said so.*

There was what sounded like a faint chuckle from the window, which then faded to silence.

Something very vague pinged at the back of Kathy's mind, something long ago . . .

But then it swirled and settled and was gone.

Kathy finished her paperwork, retrieved her handbag and coat and walked to the front door.

As always, before turning out the lights, she gave a final prim sweep with her gaze across the stacks on the first floor, up the spiral stairs to the second floor balcony, noting with satisfaction the neat short rows of shelves jutting out from the wall, empty retrieval carts in the hallway that ran along the balcony—

No, not empty—one cart was still partly full up there. She would have to talk to Marjorie on Thursday. The girl was obviously in a hormone dither, always flirting instead of doing the few things she had to do—

Something moved behind the cart.

"Who is that?" Kathy Marks snapped immediately. "Who's up there? Come out this minute!"

The cart was still as stone, and there was no sound.

And then, behind her, a dry cold sound at the window again: *Let me in . . .*

Kathy jumped, spun around and faced the nearest window. A gust of wind rattled the pane. There was no one there. She spun on her heel and caught a slight movement up on the balcony behind the cart.

"Stand up immediately!" she shouted, angry with herself that her voice sounded a bit hysterical.

As much to get away from the window as anything, she marched to the spiral staircase and mounted it, her footfalls echoing metallically as she circled higher.

She heard a scuttling sound above her, and the front window below rattled again: *Call me Sammy . . .*

Something tugged harder at her memory and sent

a chill through her. Once again, without thinking, she brushed her left forearm with her fingers.

Thoroughly rattled now, Kathy huffed in frustration and fear as she reached the landing. It gave her a view down the balcony corridor to the far wall.

There was no one behind the cart.

Sam . . .

"Stop that!" she yelled, and at the same moment saw the briefest hint of movement in the short corridor behind the cart, between two shelves.

In a second she was in front of the opening, staring in—

"What—?"

A young girl squatting on the floor held up a book protectively in front of her face, as if to ward off a blow. A backpack was beside her on the floor.

"Please don't be mad at me, Ms. Marks! I got here late, and left my library card at home, and—"

"Annabeth Turner?" the librarian replied in disbelief. She stepped forward and yanked the book out of the crouching girl's hands. The exposed face behind it was suffused with a look of remorse and terror and something else—almost defiance.

"Please don't tell my mother! Please just let me go!"

Startled by the girl's frantic reaction, Kathy softened her tone. "Just what were you doing in here? Don't you realize you would have been locked in the library overnight?" She added, in a slightly sterner voice, "Stand up this minute."

The girl did as she was told.

She looked older than her twelve years—thin, pale, almost as tall as the librarian herself, with straight brown hair cut in bangs. Her haircut, her awkwardness, her height, her way of dressing— obvious hand-me-downs at least a decade out-of-date—made her, even to Kathy Marks's less than trendy, Talbot's-styled sensibility, a walking poster girl for peer ridicule.

Something in the librarian, an echo of her own awkward and unhappy past, sympathized with the young girl. When she spoke again her tone was almost gentle. "Tell me why you tried to stay here overnight, Annabeth."

The girl stared at the floor.

"Trouble at home?" Kathy asked. "I know you haven't lived here long, but believe me, there are people in Orangefield who can help you with—"

"Nothing like that," the girl replied quickly, not looking up, which told the librarian that there may be something there after all.

"Annabeth, look at me."

The young girl raised her head slowly and Kathy blinked, startled by the intensity in her eyes. She had expected them to be full of tears, but here was that hard, defiant look again.

Recovering, Kathy said, "Is there anything you want to talk to me about? You've spent almost every day since you moved here in July in the library—first there was the astronomy section you tore through, and then the encyclopedias, and now heaven knows what else. I thought from the talks we've had that maybe we'd become friends. I know how hard it's been on you since your father died, Annabeth. You know I lost my own parents when I was your age—"

"My name is Wizard," the girl announced, "not Annabeth. I don't let anyone call me that anymore."

At a loss for words, the librarian replied, "You still haven't told me why you tried to lock yourself in here—"

"There are books you won't let me take out."

Something that had been lurking at the very back of Kathy Marks's awareness now came forward. She realized they were standing in front of the section marked LOCAL HISTORY.

"You have a project to do on Orangefield? I'm sure I could arrange—"

Her eyes still defiant, the girl answered, "Not that."

Kathy turned over the book she had taken from the girl's hand; the title read *Occult History of Orangefield* by D. A. Withers. There was a RESTRICTED stamp on the cover.

The librarian looked at the girl. "You're interested in ghosts and such?"

An almost secret smile came to the girl's lips. "You could say."

For the first time since the strange interview had started, it occurred to Kathy Marks that the girl standing before her might be on drugs, or worse.

"I want you to give me your home phone number, so I can talk to your mother," the librarian said in a sterner voice than she had yet used. She dug into her bag for the pen and notepad that were always there.

The girl said nothing, then recited the number in a curt voice.

There was a sudden loud sound below, from the

first floor. The front window with the pumpkin in it began to rattle, as if someone were rapidly knocking on it with a knuckled fist.

The librarian stared at the window, trying to see if anyone was there, but the sound abruptly stopped. When she turned back to Annabeth the girl had reached down to pick up her backpack.

"I have to go," Annabeth said. Her voice had become almost sweet, making the librarian reassess her yet again.

The awkward girl, lonely, trying to find her way, trouble at home, just like the spinster librarian.

"Will you let me check out that book?"

The librarian said, "I'm sorry, Annabeth, but I can't do that. Perhaps if you come back tomorrow, we can talk about this project of yours."

Again a sea change in the girl. She became furtive. "Maybe," she said.

She brushed by the librarian, putting on her backpack as she skipped down the metal circular stairway to the first floor. She was out the front door of the building before Kathy Marks could react.

Absently, the librarian lay *Occult History of Orangefield* in the retrieval cart; Marjorie could put it away tomorrow along with the books she'd neglected.

She was dismounting the spiral staircase, lost in thought, when another series of loud rappings came against the front window. She froze and stared in that direction.

To the side of the cutout pumpkin, Annabeth Turner's face was pressed against the glass, with the strangest look of triumph and fright on her face. She waved at the librarian and then pulled away from the glass into the night.

The librarian heard a single bark of laughter.

It wasn't until the next day that her assistant Marjorie discovered that three other restricted books, all on the occult, were missing from the Local History section.

CHAPTER THIRTY

You've done very well, Wizard.

She wanted to shout, "Thank you!"

Two blocks from the library, on an empty side street, she suddenly became short of breath. A whirling screen of dizzy images replaced her vision as she stopped dead in the street, putting her hands down to the sidewalk to steady herself, trying to calmly regain the flow of air into her lungs.

Faces, twirling pictures in orange and black, pumpkins, always pumpkins, sheeted ghosts like the white sheet she wore when she was little, a bag in her hand, two poke-holes for the eyes, the faces of mother and dead father, his face as white as the sheet, a swirl of candy corn, orange and white, a black cat filling her vision with a hiss, red tongue, white teeth and whiskers, green wild eyes and then gone, the steady feel of the sidewalk under her hands and her wheezing throat constricting . . .

Asthma attack.

She tried to even her breath, but it was too late. Knowing from experience not to move, she relaxed and raised one hand from the sidewalk while resting on the other hand and her knees. Slowly she reached around into her pack for the inhaler.

There was no air . . .

Now panic began to set in. She curled down onto the sidewalk, still rummaging in the bag and then suddenly ripping it off her shoulders, pushing it away from her arms and clawing in the front pocket . . .

The inhaler wasn't there!

And then suddenly it was—her fingers closing around it and yanking it to her mouth, she was on her back now, staring at streetlights and night sky, the sharp corner of an empty house, and with both hands she pushed the instrument into her mouth, began to breathe in slowly . . .

Breath came.

Still slowly, she pulled air in, pushing it out in little gasps and then in larger gulps as the attack subsided.

She waited for him to talk to her, but there was nothing in her head.

She stared at a scattering of stars between the corner of the house and a streetlight, a tall tree limb shorn of most of its leaves.

As if in answer, an oak leaf pirouetted down into view, landed next to her face.

She wanted to laugh.

And then cry.

"I've done well, haven't I?" she said into the night. "I've done well as Wizard?"

There was no answer.

The house was dark, but that was no surprise.

Annabeth pushed her key into the front door, opened it with a creak. The porch light overhead was off, had been since the bulb had burnt out a month ago. It had gone unreplaced. Just to make sure, she checked the switch on the inside wall—it was off, as she had expected, and when she jiggled it on nothing happened. There was another switch next to the outside light and she flipped it up, turning on a single lamp on the far side of the living room.

The room was a mess, as always—magazines, newspapers scattered, unpacked boxes, a nest of cat hair on one sidechair where their feline slept, furniture, mantle, a few knickknacks all undusted. The rug was stained, soiled, hadn't been vacuumed in weeks. Under the single lamp was an ashtray full of cigarette butts, a nearly empty tumbler with clear liquid nesting the bottom, a single ice cube almost extinct.

This is what you get when you have nothing.

With no expectations, Annabeth walked past the stairway back to the kitchen, which was in similar disarray—stacked dishes, a vague ammonia smell battling the odor of soured milk, a broken dish on the sideboard kept from tumbling into the sink by a half-eaten sandwich perched on the sink's edge, a full garbage can blocking the door to the backyard. The overhead fluorescent light, a round, naked white curl whose ornamental glass cover had long disappeared, flickered fitfully and never quite blossomed on.

The short hallway behind the kitchen was lined with dust bunnies, two unmatching shoes side-by-side in the center, incongruous.

Loud snoring came from the bedroom at the end of the hall, the door of which was ajar. As she stopped, Annabeth sensed movement, saw Ludwig, their cat, staring out at her balefully from the end of the rumpled bed.

Her mother made an interrupted snoring sound and turned away toward the wall.

Annabeth retreated to the stairway and climbed up to the other bedroom, her own. Within there was another world. The walls were freshly painted, the floors dusted, the throw rug bright with its original colors. The desk beneath the single window was tidy, one side stacked with schoolbooks, the other, in front of the cane-backed chair, fronted with a clean blotter and a neat row of pens and pencils. The bed was crisply made, covered with a quilt showing a shower of yellow stars and moons against a deep blue background. Over the bed was a single poster, framed, not thumbtacked, of a white observatory dome, its slit open, revealing the huge telescope within pointed at the night sky. It had been a stop-motion shot, the shutter kept open for hours while the stars revolved in the sky, and they formed streaked halos around the dome.

Annabeth's own telescope, a sleek white tube four inches in diameter and nearly three feet long, mounted on a sturdy wooden tripod, stood vigil beside the bed. Against the wall behind it was a bookcase crammed with astronomy books and fantasy novels.

Annabeth put her backpack on the bed, opened it and drew out the three stolen library books from inside it. She put them on the blotter on her desk, facedown. She leaned over them to look out the window.

Above the huge oak tree in the backyard there was a scattering of stars, but clouds were already moving up from the western horizon into the chill night, and there was a waxing moon still high enough to wash out whatever would be visible.

She could just make out the Great Square of the constellation Pegasus, and, next to it, the constellation Andromeda, which, along its split lines, contained the only galaxy outside the Milky Way visible to the naked eye. She could just make out its faint oval blush. In her telescope, it was a magnificent cloud possessing billions of stars far beyond our own galactic neighborhood.

It was said that our own galaxy would someday crash into it.

That, she had decided before coming to Orangefield, was where her dead father's soul was.

Her father's soul, along with all the others, was in the Andromeda Galaxy, which would one day crash into our own galaxy, and bring all the dead back.

That had been her belief

Now she no longer believed it—she believed other things instead. Things that might actually be true.

She turned from the window and looked down at the stack of stolen library books on her blotter.

She turned back to the window and located the Andromeda galaxy again.

"I promise," she said to the Andromeda galaxy, to her father, to the other billions of souls in that hazy oval of false heaven, "that I'll find you. I promise."

She pulled the shade down over the window, sat down at the desk, and turned over the first book: *Halloween in Orangefield*.

On the front cover had been stamped the word: RESTRICTED.

She opened it up; the binding didn't crack the way an unused book's would—this opening was smooth, the latest of many.

Good, Wizard. Good, the returning voice in her head spoke.

"Everything was fine before he died. You promised when you first made me Wizard three weeks ago—"

And I'll keep my promise, Wizard, if you do what I say.

She smiled to herself and turned the page.

CHAPTER THIRTY-ONE

As far as the eye could see.

The Pumpkin Tender woke up and was nearly blinded by autumn colors. There was moisture on his clothes and face, and he shivered as he sat up. The ground had been hard the night before, under the sickle moon, but overnight it had softened beneath him with dew. He had been foolish not to use the Army blanket, one of his only possessions, along with his felt hat and leather boots and his rabbit's foot. As if to answer his own fear, he reached into his pocket and felt the soft length of the good luck charm. He immediately calmed enough to rub his eyes and really wake up.

The sun was resting on the eastern oaks, which meant it was seven A.M. or so. The sky was autumn blue and cloudless; later the sun would climb and warm the dew back into the air, and it would probably be in the sixties in the afternoon.

He wondered if this would be the day.

He wouldn't have long to find out.

He had chosen to sleep in a low hollow, one of the shallow valleys just outside the town limits, and that had been a foolish thing. He had done many foolish things lately, which vaguely bothered him. Some of the memories crowded into his head, and he pushed them out, physically driving them back with his hands, making agitated sounds with his mouth.

He closed his eyes and the memories were gone.

Frankenstein, the kids in Orangefield called him, because he was big and wore shabby clothes and had rough hands and could no longer talk.

Not since . . .

Again he became agitated and looked to the sun for help. It was above the trees now, free of them, climbing. In another hour or two it would show him what he lived to see.

The only thing he lived for. That and the other thing . . .

The worst memory of all came into his head and now he cried out, making the same sounds Frankenstein made in that movie he saw before the Army. He could speak then, and walk without the bad hitch in his right leg. Sometimes he almost had clear memories of the way he had been before the Army, when he drove a '64 Mustang convertible, which he'd restored himself, and smoked cigarettes and drank beer and was on the bowling team at Ace's and there was that girl Peggy . . .

His loud sounds turned to mewling and he sat

down facing the sun. He found his Army blanket at his feet and pulled it up around him.

He had been another man before the Army. The training he remembered, Fort Bragg, shipping out, Somalia, but all of it was speeded up like a film in fast forward with a cartoon *whirring* sound that got higher and higher pitched until it stopped dead on the moment his foot was resting on the antipersonnel mine and froze there, his eyes looking down and his brain screaming *What the hell?* even as his weight lifted off the mine and it went off, and his leg, his thigh, his hip were blown to bits.

He knew that wasn't quite right, that there was more, but that he couldn't quite remember. . . .

He had a feeling if he did it would make things even worse.

Feels like someone tearing the meat up off my bones was the last rational thought he had before a piece of his own ankle bone ripped into his mouth and then up through his palate, severing his tongue on the way, stopping in his brain.

"Kid made his own bullet," one of the field doctors said later, laughing in that sardonic, funeral parlor way MASH doctors had, and even now part of him wanted to laugh the same way when he remembered that.

Then he came home and after a while was *Frankenstein*.

No more Peggy, no siree, not with three quarters of a brain and no tongue and a hitch in his walk bigger than Festus on TV. . . .

He watched the sun climb ever higher—he'd know when it was time—but already he felt it warming the wet off him.

No more Aaron Peters, he'd had a tongue and a good leg and a girlfriend and a car and liked to read history books. A pretty good pitching arm, too, and not a bad quarterback for a lefty.

He became, instead, Frankenstein.

And the Pumpkin Tender.

Peggy married a guy named Turk, who laid a hand on her now and then, he heard someone say. The same someone said it was a shame, that Aaron would have made a wonderful husband.

Maybe it was his mother who said that, he wasn't sure. . . .

His kid brother took the Mustang and wrapped it around a pole six months after Aaron got back, walking away from the wreck. In a way the Pumpkin Tender was glad the car was gone. One thing less to think about when he looked at it, memories firing off like pistons in his broken head.

He knew they were uncomfortable when he was home, so he'd started staying away as much as he could, and took care of their guilt at least in the summer and fall when old Joshua Froelich hired him to weed and tend his pumpkin patch.

"Better'n a dog," Froelich had said, since Aaron tended Froelich's land like a hawk on legs, killing anything—weed, insect or animal—that went after the pumpkins. Soon word about this wonder had spread, and the Pumpkin Tender found himself taking care of most of the pumpkins in Orangefield. In the winter he stayed mostly at home, making them all nervous and irritable, becoming Frankenstein, but in the spring, after the last snow, he began to wander the still fallow fields that surrounded the town like a wreath, pulling up rocks that had been forced up through the frozen ground, cleaning out dead vines and late weeds he had missed the previous autumn, making his fields ready for planting. By the time planting came in the summer he lived in the fields, tending each shoot like a baby and nurturing each budded fruit as if it were the only one in the world. The pumpkins he tended were the best grown, the cleanest, the fattest, brightest-colored, longest-lasting-after-picking, finest in all of the Northeast. Froelich and the other growers had customers drive two hundred miles just to buy one of those pumpkins.

The Pumpkin Tender had become indispensable.

And perhaps today would be the one day in the year he would be truly happy.

He thought it might be. The way the sun was rising, the cleaness of the atmosphere, the cool snap in the air, gave him hope. It would have to be today, because he felt rain behind this weather, which meant that tomorrow was the day he would lose it.

He stood up.

No, today was the day. He was sure.

He left the Army blanket in a heap and began the long, limping trek to the High Spot. He didn't think about this. Like an animal drawn to a spawning ground, he took step after step toward his goal.

His leg began to ache after a half hour, but he ignored it. He passed Froelich's farm stand, passing behind the building so he wouldn't have to interact with the old man, but Froelich was in the back, unloading potato sacks from the back of his pickup truck.

"This the day, Aaron?" the old man said, stopping his work. He was overweight and already perspiring.

Aaron nodded curtly and limped on.

There was an understanding tone in Froelich's voice. "Maybe I'll join you up there later, after you've been alone with it awhile."

The Pumpkin Tender made a sound in the back of his throat and kept walking. Froelich had never joined him, and was just being polite.

The sun was higher now and the sky was an achingly clear blue. The chill had dissipated. It would be even warmer than he thought—maybe up into the low seventies. Nothing like it had been in early October, but still nice for this time of year.

He took his felt hat off his head with his left hand, mopped his sweaty face with it and pushed it back onto his head.

The ground was now steadily ascending.

Already, if he turned around he would be above the valleys that surrounded Orangefield. Beyond those valleys were either softly rolling hills or a few higher spots, only one of which could be considered a mountain. It wasn't tall enough to be named, but was high enough to afford a view of the entire area.

Halfway up the mountain, and by his reading of the sun just before noon, he stopped. His leg from the hip to his rebuilt ankle was on fire. He sat down in a hollow under a tree; the spot was filled with red and gold leaves and he was able to nest down into it and stretch his leg out.

He was thirsty and hungry, but had neither food nor water. There was a stream a little way on, but he had been warned not to drink from it—the one time he had done so his stomach had been turned inside out for three days.

The red and gold leaves made him think of fire, of his leg burning in them. The leaves began to remind him of flame itself, of the burning up his leg and the ripping sound of his own flesh being torn away, and he reached down and brushed all the leaves away from his legs.

He was facing away from the sun.

His leg began to feel better, a lessening of the fire, and he lay back and became comfortable in the warmth and the lessening of pain. He closed his eyes, and soon fell asleep.

He dreamed, and for once the dream was almost a pleasant one to begin with, blue and white and he was in the clouds, flying above a flaming earth, none of the heat reaching him. It was cool and he was comfortable and floated with no effort or fear.

And then the world below him went suddenly dark and the fires went away without leaving smoke, and the clouds were gone and the sky around him became darker and darker, and he was surrounded by black and cold and was falling, trying to scream and nothing came out—

He awoke with a start and called out from his ruined mouth. For a moment he was disoriented. He heard a crackling sound, and felt leaves behind his head and saw his legs in the cleared-out spot.

He became very agitated—the light around him was deeper than it should be.

Alarmed, he stood up, feeling a fresh hot bolt of pain through his leg. He ignored it. He hobbled out of the hollow spot, onto the path again, and faced the sun.

It was past its height and moving down in its arc toward the west in the late of day. And in the west clouds were already forming on the line of the horizon, rising like yeast to meet the approaching sun.

He had slept for hours.

He wanted to cry. He had missed the height of the sun.

Steeling himself, he turned to the upward path and limped onto it. Perhaps it was not too late.

His leg quickly became a pure hot pain with each step. He gritted his teeth and ignored it. After a while he heard an anguished sound, which fell into step with him—he realized the cries were his own loud grunts at the pace he'd set.

But he could now see the summit above him, growing closer with each burning step.

He came around a bend in the path beside a stand of leafless trees and saw the flat top of the mountain twenty yards ahead.

His leg folded under him and he fell.

A sound like a strangled cry came from his mouth. His leg felt as if it had been dipped into acid. He tried to get up, but fell back again.

The sun was descending toward the west, darkening the late autumn day—soon it would be twilight.

He tried again to rise, and failed. He began to sob.

Suddenly there were hands beneath his armpits, pulling him up. "Can't have you missin' your favorite day of the year, can we, Aaron?"

He was on his feet, and supported. He turned to see old Froelich's face next to his own.

The old man looked suddenly embarrassed at the intimacy and turned away. But his grip on Aaron was like iron. "Don't worry 'bout it, son. Just thought you were in an extra bit of difficulty with the leg this year, when you went by the stand. Thought it was time I see this sight myself, anyways. So I took the truck up as far as I could, walked the rest. Thought you'd be up and gone by now. And if you weren't . . ." He shrugged, looked Aaron in the face again. "Let's have us a look, shall we?"

With the old man's help, the Pumpkin Tender suddenly found himself on top of the mountain, looking down at the valleys that surrounded Orangefield—the scores of pumpkin fields and patches that merged into an orange circle, a ring of fire, the sight of thousands of unpicked pumpkins in the late sun. It was even more magnificent than it would have been at noon—the deep tone of setting Sol making the fields seem to be lit from within.

"Well, I'll be damned, I will," old Froelich said in amazement. "I had no idea it would be this beautiful, Aaron. And it's all your doing, boy. All those clean, beautiful pumpkins yet to be picked . . ." He laughed. "Hell, we could sell tickets to this, it's so beautiful."

There were tears in the Pumpkin Tender's eyes. His mouth opened and a little gasping sound came out.

"That's all right, son," Froelich said, tightening his grip under Aaron's arms. "You just stand there and enjoy it. Hell, it's gonna rain tomorrow, and then picking in earnest will start. This'll all be gone for another year."

The sun sank into imperceptible twilight, and the ring of fire's glow faded like cooling embers.

"I'll be damned," the old farmer repeated, his voice fading like the light.

They stood together silently for a moment; the sun dropped into the clouded horizon, the glow disappearing, the light dying.

"Come on, son," Froelich said, trying to urge the Pumpkin Tender to turn away. "Time we went back down. The truck's just a little ways down the path."

Aaron wouldn't move. There were tears on his face, and his weight caused the old man to let go of his grip and gently lower him to the ground.

"Gonna stay up here tonight, Aaron?" Froelich asked. He knew from experience not to try to fight the Pumpkin Tender's impulses. "All right, then. Just in case, I went and got your spare Army blanket from the spot in the shed where you keep your stuff. It's in the truck, let me get it."

The old man wandered off down the path, returned a few minutes later.

Aaron, on the ground, his legs folded awkwardly, felt the blanket go around his shoulders.

"You take care up here, boy. Try to rest that leg of yours."

Aaron heard the old man's steps retreat, heard the rumbling roar of the truck's engine a few moments later—the protesting grind of changed gears, the crunch of tires turning. Headlights stabbed through the growing dark above his head, then arced away. In a moment he heard the truck change gears again, the fading sound of its engine as it made its rumbling way down the mountain.

He was alone with the coming night. Already the line of clouds in the west had eaten the sun, were climbing up the sky, swallowing early stars.

The ring of fire around Orangefield, which now blinked on its own electric lights against the night, was gone.

Tears continued to dry on the Pumpkin Tender's face. His hands beneath the blanket gripped and ungripped.

Inside his head the voice, the same voice that had been talking to him since Froelich had lifted him up, had continued to talk to him insistently, soothingly, with command; as he had tried to enjoy the ring of fire of his own making, it still talked to him. It was the clearest thing he had heard since Somalia, and he knew if it kept up he would listen to it.

Remember me? it said.

CHAPTER THIRTY-TWO

Lists.

While he buried the headless animal, Jordie thought about all the lists he kept. There was the comic book list—his favorites, beginning with *The Fantastic Four* and ending, at the very bottom, with *Batman*. There was a lot in between, but *Batman* was the only DC title in the bunch, and just barely. He had liked the movies more than the books, but there was something about the character that he just couldn't dismiss. Maybe it was the fact that Batman was just a man with a neat suit. No super powers, no glowing rocks, no super-speed—just a man with a mission.

Man with a mission.

Jordie kept lots of other lists: lists of what to get at the store, of what parts he needed to order for his turntables—needles, especially, he needed new needles for his cartridges, his vinyl was starting to sound a bit distorted—a list of what needed to be done around the house. That was the one he hated the most, but one, now that he thought about it, that he didn't have to bother with anymore. Mom and Aunt Binny had worked long and hard on that one—but, well, he just wouldn't bother with it anymore.

The animal's torso was covered with dirt; he wondered idly if he'd dug deep enough, but decided that, hell, that sounded too much like a chore, so what he'd done was good enough.

"You don't work, you don't go to school, you don't do anything around the house," his mother was fond of saying.

"Look, Ma, I'm doin' a chore!" he said, giggling.

Man, it was cold. He looked down at himself and saw that he was naked, smeared with blood. The sun had gone down. It had still been up when he started digging, but now it was dark and getting chilly. It had been warm as hell a few weeks ago, but now it was really October. He stood up, dropped the shovel and dusted his hands, turning toward the house.

Lists.

There was something else he was supposed to do.

He looked down on the ground, looking for the list, but couldn't locate it. He shrugged, walked into the house, turning lights on as he went. He had a joint somewhere—where was it? He couldn't remember. He vaguely remembered smoking three or four in the morning, the afternoon. And there had been a pint of vodka in there somewhere, or had it been a fifth . . .

The house was a mess, kitchen chairs turned over,

table on its side, blood smears on the white floors, walls, refrigerator, everywhere. The head of a cat stared at him from the kitchen counter next to the toaster oven. Another, larger head was next to it. A second animal, what looked like a mouse but was actually a squirrel, lay eviscerated on the toaster oven's open door.

He laughed.

The rest of the house was a mess, too—some broken furniture, the couch with a burn mark in the center cushion, a scatter of feathers in the fireplace . . .

The bathroom, at least, was clean.

He took a slow shower, letting warm and then hot water sluice over him, scrubbing himself with Ivory soap. He still couldn't remember what the other list had said. He knew he should, but his head was just too cloudy.

He let hot, steamy water run onto his face, onto his shaggy head of hair.

Got to remember, got to . . .

It almost came to him, then danced off into the back of his mind again. Finally, he shut off the water with an angry, squeaky turn of the handle, got out of the shower and stood before the mirror.

Lettered on the steamed surface in a bold hand was: IN YOUR ROOM.

"Yeah?" he said, out loud.

Then, in his head, the voice fighting through all the static: *Go to your room, Jordie.*

He shrugged. "Whatever."

Not bothering to towel himself off, he padded out

of the bathroom, pushing aside a broken end table that had somehow found its way in front of his bedroom, and opened the door.

The usual mess inside, nothing more: unmade bed, records scattered on the floor, a pair of Timberlake boots in front of the open, cluttered closet, his turntables neat and clean on their industrial-sized folding table flanking stacked amps and a mixer, huge JBL dj speakers to either side on the carpeted floor.

He switched the rig on, forgetting about the voice, the list.

The amp hummed into life and he opened the turn covers; one already had an LP on it, gangster rap, and he slapped an R&B record pulled at random from the nearest sleeve onto the other.

He let the rap record dash into its angry opening, then abruptly switched over with the mixer to the mild rhythm and blues record. Snorting satisfaction, he kept it there, a soft crooning voice flowing from the excellent speakers.

"Awwright!"

Find the list, Jordie.

"Right. Sure."

And there it was, right in front of him, on top of the amp, taped down and neat as can be. Next to it was another piece of paper, looked older, folded over and taped closed.

At the bottom of the list was: *Mom*, followed by *Aunt Binny*, then a list of large animals ascending to *Cat* and *Squirrel* at the top.

So that had been what he was burying—the cat's body.

Rusty, his name was.

Had been.

You didn't listen to me, Jordie.

Jordie shrugged, hardly listening; he was mouthing the words of the R&B song.

You didn't follow my directions.

The needle abruptly scratched all the way across the surface of the vinyl, then lifted by itself and was set firmly in its cradle.

Jordie watched this in horror, complained, "Hey! Those things cost money!"

The amp switched itself off.

Listen to me, Jordie.

"Bullshi—"

The electrical cord from the amp pulled itself from the back of the machine, frayed into two separate wires, touched Jordie's still dripping leg.

A shock went through him, up his body into his neck.

He found himself on the floor, trembling, a raw red welt on his leg where the wires had touched.

Listen.

"Yeah, okay." His voice was weak, suddenly frightened.

Get dressed.

"Sure. Whatever you say."

Yes, Jordie, whatever I say. From now on.

He dressed quickly—jeans, shirt, Timberlakes.

Take the list. Go into the living room.

Head clear now, hands still trembling, Jordie reached for the taped, closed list on the amp.

Not that one. The first one.

"Sure." Jodie took the original list.

Now go into the living room and clean up.

"Right." He stumbled out of his bedroom, down the hall and into the living room.

His mother's headless body was in front of the couch, Aunt Binny's body sprawled in a wing chair facing the fireplace.

You were supposed to start at the top *of the list, Jordie. Not the bottom.*

"Huh?"

And I told you to spread it out over the next few days, ease into it slowly.

"Really?"

I didn't expect you to be so . . . eager. And so fast.

Jordie shrugged idly. "Whatever."

That's not good enough. I'm going to give you a second chance, but I want you to do everything I say. Do you agree?

Jordie heard the sound of something sliding up the hallway, looked to see the electrical cord, two bare wires poised like a coiled python in the opening to the living room. The other end of the cord slid into view like a snake and plugged itself with a *snick* into a wall outlet just inside the room.

"Gotcha. Whatever you say."

Go back into your bedroom and look at the second list taped to your amp.

"Sure. Right away."

Jordie moved out of the room, giving the electrical cord a wide berth—its bare-wired ends, like slitted copper eyes hanging in the air, followed his movements.

He stumbled backward into his room, went to the amp and pulled off the second list.

Open it up.

"No problem."

The electrical cord had followed him, was in the doorway, watching.

He opened the piece of paper, stared at it. It had been folded many times, was creased through some of the writing, which had faded it. Its edges were frayed. It was in a different hand than the other list, which, now that he concentrated on it, he remembered writing himself.

Read it, Jordie. Out loud.

This one was in his mother's hand. He remembered that now, the careful penmanship. She had written this note for him a long time ago.

Read it now, Jordie. The voice was impatient.

"Remember to take your meds, Jordie," he read. "Remember the doses." Then there was a list underneath, various doses each of various pills, names like *Clozaril*, *Zoloft*, *Lithium*, *Zyprexa*, as well as the times he needed to take them.

The note was signed, *Love, Mom.*

I want you to begin to take your meds again, Jordie. Only in slightly different doses.

"But you told me to stop—"

Yes. And now I want you to start again, in the doses I

tell you to take. They'll make you . . . receptive, and happy. And now I want you to clean up. I want you to clean up so no one will know.

"Sure thing."

I'll tell you how to take your meds from now on.

He held up the note in his hand. "But my mom—"

Just listen to me from now on. You don't need that list anymore. Get rid of it. From now on I'll make lists for you.

Jordie stared at the note in his hand for a moment—*Love, Mom*—and then crumpled it up and let it drop to the floor.

Very good, Jordie.

Jordie saw with relief that the electrical cord had dropped to the hallway floor and lay curled and dead.

When you're finished cleaning up, the voice said, *I want you to sleep. Then I'll have a new list for you. To-morrow, you can decorate the house for Halloween.*

CHAPTER THIRTY-THREE

On page twenty-one of the second of the three books she had stolen from the Orangefield Library, *A Short History of Halloween*, Annabeth Turner found what she was looking for:

> *Samhain, the Celtic Lord of Death—whose celebration day was also known as Samhain—had the power to return the souls of the dead to their earthly homes temporarily. Often, though not always, this occurred on one special evening—the evening that eventually became known in the Christian era as All Hallows Eve.*

So that's who he was. *Call me Sam.*

She looked up from the book, out through the window over her desk, but there was no answer.

She turned back to the book.

She knew she had only tonight to learn whatever

she could from the three books. *Halloween in Orange-field* had proved useless; the usual local historian twaddle, written to titillate visitors and tourists without telling them anything of historical import. It was little more than a children's book, and she wondered why it had been in the restricted area at all.

A Short History of Halloween must have been placed in the Local History section by mistake, but had proved at least of some use—but besides its discussion of the Celts, and their Lord of Death, it had quickly veered away into modern practices.

She put it aside and opened the third book.

The spine cracked with disuse—she wondered if she was the first to ever open the book and saw by the librarian's card in the front that it had never been taken out.

The title was *Occult Practices in Orangefield and Chicawa County, New York, 1668–1940.*

She looked at the copyright page and saw that it had only recently been published, and that a second volume, covering 1941 to the present, was promised by the publisher, who was also the author: T.R. Reynolds.

She turned to the first page of text.

Immediately she was disappointed—it was illustrated with a picture of the Salem witch trials, a solemn woodcut of three witches being burned at the stake. Annabeth was a good, fast reader, and skimmed through the accompanying description of the Salem hysteria; her eyes stopped when she reached the following:

It isn't generally recognized that a similar episode of hysteria occurred in Orangefield, New York, the previous spring, predating the Salem madness by almost a year. What makes the Orangefield episode doubly interesting—and makes it doubly curious that it has for so long been ignored—is that a total of fourteen women and three men were condemned as agents of the devil, and that ten of them in all—eight of the women and two men— were executed either by hanging or stoning. Perhaps because none were burned at the stake this episode has been generally forgotten, both in local lore and in the larger picture of witch hysteria which gripped the eastern colonies during that short, strange period.

Annabeth skimmed ahead, flying past numerous supposed "possessions" and, during the Civil War, a mass disappearance of local men, which the author tried to relate to an earlier Virginia episode but which turned out to be a wholesale avoidance of Union Army conscription.

The rest of the book, as she moved through it quickly, looked to be composed of similar stories, many of which were backed up by nothing but hearsay and gossip.

She was about to give up on the book when she moved to the last chapter: "The Pumpkinfield Era and the Beginning of 'Samhain Sightings.'"

The chapter was fronted by a black-and-white photograph of a field of pumpkins, row after row nearly to the horizon, with a caption that read: "First pumpkin farm in 'Pumpkinfield,' 1940."

Once again she skimmed, learning that during the early part of the Great Depression the name of the town, as a publicity gimmick, had been briefly changed to Pumpkinfield. When the name change produced little increase in tourist traffic, it was changed back to Orangefield. By this time word had spread about the size and quality of the local pumpkins, and this, more than any gimmick, is what finally made the town prosperous.

But by 1940, after the town had regained its original name, a curious phenomenon had begun: sightings, around Halloween, of a dark, cloaked figure appearing in pumpkin fields, usually at night, which the locals dubbed "Samhain Sightings." There didn't seem to be any specific origin for the sightings, and the author had, by his own admission, been unable to discover why the name Samhain had become attached to the mysterious figure.

She thought of the Pumpkin Boy for a moment, then shook her head and read on. No, the Pumpkin Boy had been real, a machine. This was something else.

There followed the same short description of the Celtic Death Lord—and and the pagan rituals that had attended him on All Hallows Eve—which *A Short History of Halloween* had provided.

But then there was this:

In October of 1941, just before the onset of World War II, there occurred in Orangefield an unprece-

dented rash of sightings of what the locals now referred to as 'Sam.' Up until that point the name had been used with an almost cheerful irreverence (see notes, pp. 124–126, interviews with Mattie Michaels, etc.) which mirrored that of the residents of Loch Ness, in Scotland, who affectionately call their lake creature Nessie. But after the incidents of 1941 things changed, and to this day the name Samhain is almost never spoken of lightly in Orangefield, even in jest. It is rare to hear the phenomenon referred to as Sam anymore.

There followed a few descriptions of early Sam sightings, usually of a tall, darkly cloaked, mute figure who appeared in the middle of a pumpkin patch on moonlit nights; the sightings became more numerous as Halloween approached, and continued even after a prankster from a nearby town was caught impersonating Samhain.

In a sidebar, it was noted that the impersonator was later found hanged, and that it was never determined whether or not it had been a suicide.

Even this, Reynolds admits, might have ended the matter if two grizzly murders hadn't occurred on Halloween of that year; the bodies, of a teenaged girl and boy, had been found hacked to pieces in a pumpkin patch. There were unidentified shoe prints near the bodies, and the murders were never solved.

After that, the name Sam, or Samhain, was never spoken in Orangefield. The murders, allied to other strange occurrences that fall and winter, which was

*a harsh one, conspired to turn Sam from a local leg-
end into something taboo. There were economic as
well as cultural reasons for this, no doubt—if people were scared of a black-cloaked murderer, they
wouldn't come to Orangefield for the pumpkins or
the foliage, and they wouldn't spend their money
there. That, and the fact that Pearl Harbor was
bombed five weeks after Halloween and the murders, turned local interests to more solid and national pursuits. Indeed, by the end of the war, the
Sam phenomenon had all but been forgotten, and
there were no more sightings until 1951, a period
which will be discussed in the second volume of this
history, which will also cover the bizarre occurrences surrounding Orangefield's annual Pumpkin
Days Festival, initiated in 1952 and held every year
during the week leading up to Halloween.*

The book abruptly ended at that point, leaving
Annabeth both satisfied and frustrated. She wanted
to know more—wanted to know *all* of it. She
searched in vain for some indication of when the
second volume would be published, but found
nothing—there wasn't even a picture of the author
on the back cover.

She turned to the copyright page again, noting the
publisher's address: Reynolds Publishing, 1420 Acre
Street, Orangefield. She wrote it down.

Sleep tugged at her, and she readied for bed and
slipped under the covers. The room was cold, and
she pulled the star-covered quilt up to her chin. To-

morrow she would return the three books to the library when Ms. Marks, the librarian, wasn't there. She'd learned everything she could from the library, anyway.

You're doing well, Wizard.

The voice was in her head, just as it had been at the library this afternoon. There was almost laughter in it.

"Sam? Is that you?" she whispered.

Perhaps. We'll meet when the time is right. Be patient.

"But I want to know everything! I want—"

We all want things. There are things you will do for me. Then you will get what you want, as I promised.

In the dark, she felt the most insubstantial caress of fingers across her face. She reached out, but there was nothing solid there, just the merest hint of vapor. The fingers touched her own, grasping them for a fraction of a second before the vapor melted away.

The faintest of kisses brushed her lips—she smelled nutmeg and allspice, a hint of cloves. There was almost a face, white and wide, shimmering, deep sockets with no eyes, a mouth opened in an oval, a thin red-lipped grin, which puffed apart into mist.

Soon, Wizard . . .

"You promised—"

There were tears on her face, sobs threatening to well up from within her.

I know what I promised, the voice said. *Go to sleep.*

"I want to know where he is. . . ."

She closed her eyes and slept a dreamless sleep.

PART IV

PUMPKIN DAYS

CHAPTER THIRTY-FOUR

Pumpkins.

Everywhere pumpkins. Orangefield became an orange town.

If you had watched from the sky, you would have seen a remarkable thing. In mid-October, Orangefield was surrounded by a glorious ring of orange, a corona of pumpkin patches and cultivated fields, fruit so clean and bright they seemed to glow. And then the ring began to contract, the farthest layers melting inward toward the town itself. The farthest fields were picked first, fat pumpkins suddenly appearing on farm stand shelves and PICK YOUR OWN PUMPKIN signs springing up like toadstools on roadsides. And the ring continued to contract. By the third week in October it was half as thick as it had been, and now orange began to fill the town of Orangefield.

By the fourth week in the month the ring was all

but gone, a few spots of orange, a rotted or trampled pumpkin here and there, a few that grew too small to pick, or too large and oddly shaped to sell. The farm stands were bursting with fruit now, the roadside stands top heavy with pumpkins—glorious round fat fruit that *smelled* orange.

And Orangefield was filled with pumpkins. Pumpkins everywhere.

By the morning of the beginning of Pumpkin Days, Orangefield from the air was as orange as its corona of pumpkin fields had been. There was orange everywhere. Every house had a porchful of pumpkins—on some houses, the foundations all the way around the house were lined with orange fruit. Every mailbox had a pumpkin guarding its post; backyards and front were guarded by scarecrows with pumpkin heads. Every front window was filled with pumpkin cutouts; each door bore another, larger cardboard pumpkin face.

In front of Rainer Park, in the middle of town, the viewing stand was draped in orange bunting. The pumpkin floats would parade by here, and behind the grandstand were the tables lined with hundreds of the best pumpkins for the carving competition. The telephone poles were topped with plastic pumpkins; City Hall sported its orange and white banner proclaiming WELCOME PUMPKIN DAYS FESTIVAL! And under it the mayor's name in as bold letters as he dared display. He would ride the first float and open the ceremonies himself.

And more pumpkins. And more.

An orange stripe down Main Street in washable

paint. And Orange Men, the gaggle of college students who spray painted themselves orange each year; one, after too much beer, inevitably used real paint. And orange costumes—the best imitation of a pumpkin, various grades. And of course the orange and white-striped tent in the park itself, with all its wares for sale and school projects displayed: the science of pumpkin growing, things made with pumpkins (a pair of shoes!), hundreds of uses for pumpkins.

Then the baked goods and recipe displays—pumpkin cake and bread, and pies, of course, and cookies and pumpkin ale (the college students, again) and pumpkin milk and pumpkin juice. An entire meal made of pumpkin, from something resembling chicken (strips of rind from near the skin, boiled in chicken stock and then broiled) and something else resembling mashed potatoes, and things that looked like carrots and cucumbers and even peas, with pumpkin tea and pumpkin ice cream for dessert. Pumpkin ravioli and soup and sausage. Pumpkin pancakes, waffles. Pumpkin french toast, made with pumpkin bread. Not to mention the music tent, solid orange.

Orange everywhere.

Pumpkins everywhere.

Pumpkin Days, Orangefield in its glory—with attendant tourist dollars.

From the decimated corona, the battlefield after the war, the now fallow fields surrounding Orangefield, the Pumpkin Tender heard the celebrations, muted.

He never attended the festival, had never even thought much of it before Somalia. Now he stayed away as a religion. There were his trampled fields to tend, the forgotten fruit, too small or too large or too strange, which had been left behind. This was one of his favorite times, after the viewing of the orange corona. He had been in hiding since the violence had been done, and now he was left alone to fix the damage.

And collect his own special pumpkins.

He didn't mind the strange-shaped fruit, the elongated shapes that resembled huge orange egg-plants, the too-thin, the tiny, the massive squat shapes that looked like hassocks. The double pump-kins, twins growing together. Even triplets, attached at the same stem.

All day he collected them from the various fields and brought them all to one of Froelich's smaller patches. And always, as the day wore on, the rau-cous sounds coming from Orangefield and its Pumpkin Days.

By nightfall he had nearly filled the small patch with these freak fruits, and had enough to create a miniature of the fields he had tended for so many months.

In Orangefield the lights went on, the festival con-tinued as it would for the next week: the night pa-rade, the march of the pumpkins, more eating, more music, more judging.

The glow from the town made the Pumpkin Ten-der's patch glow with an orange warmth. The moon, waxing fat, rose in back of the field, giving a colder light. The Pumpkin Tender sat down in front of his patch, pulled his Army blanket around him and sat quietly.

There was a large pumpkin in front of him, which had not been picked but had been growing in this patch; it was deformed into two lobes near the bottom, but the upper part was perfect, round and firm with a strong life-giving vine still in the ground. He would keep this one alive until Thanksgiving, at least.

But now, he noticed abruptly, there was something wrong with it.

Though it hadn't been picked, somehow it had been carved and now sported a two-toothed grin, triangle eyes and nose.

A fire, not moonlight, flared up within it, and the smile widened.

Time for us to talk, Aaron, it said.

Behind it, in the middle of the patch, something dark rose up from the ground—cloaked, tall, with a hidden face.

The Pumpkin Tender looked at the fat, lobed, still-growing pumpkin again—it was back to normal, had no carved face, was smooth and untouched.

Time for us to talk.

This time the voice came from the dark-cloaked figure, which was suddenly closer, standing over him. It smelled cold, like the night, and, faintly, like pumpkin pie spice.

Aaron remembered the voice—it was the *Remember me?* voice.

He remembered other things, which he didn't want to . . .

You haven't listened to me yet, the voice said, *but now I think you will.*

And the cloak covered him.

And he screamed.

CHAPTER THIRTY-FIVE

"Did you notice anything weird at Jordie's house?" Will Coppel asked. He drained the last drops from his fifth beer and crushed the can, dropping it into the pile in the midst of the four boys.

The other three laughed, and Josh Hammer said, "Weird? That dude is *always* weird. Always was."

Will fished behind him into the cooler, felt his hand slip into bone-chilling water as he searched for another beer. His hand hit one, two beers, and he snagged the third as it swam by.

"I'm not joking," he said as he popped the tab. "You know how Jordie has to keep those medications he takes balanced. He's acting like they're all screwed up. And by the way, we're almost out of beer."

A collective groan went up. Behind them, inside the music festival tent, a circus-sized temporary structure at one end of Rainer Park, rap music burst into the night again; the break was over, and now it was the turn of the third and fourth of their group to groan again and go back inside and help the dj.

One of them turned before climbing under the tent flap. "That leaves you two to get more brews," he said.

Josh pushed the cooler into a hidden spot beneath some nearby bushes and stood up. "Forget driving," he said, "I've had too many."

"Me too," Will replied. "Got your ID?"

Josh fished in the front pocket of his pants, produced a card. "Phony as Dolly Parton's tits," he laughed. "I can't believe we're twenty years old and can't buy a beer without lying about it."

"Let's walk to Burrita's," Will replied. He glanced blurrily at his watch. "Ten to eleven. He's open till midnight, right?"

"I don't remember," Josh answered. "Might be eleven tonight."

They set off through the park, in the direction of the main road. The night was still misty with the remnants of the night's fireworks display; there would be another on the last night of Pumpkin Days, next Saturday. In between, there would be nightly music in the tent. Tonight it was rap music's turn; another night, classic rock and then classical, with the high school band filling in another night and a polka party yet another.

"You ever think about how stupid all this Pumpkin Days crap is?" Josh laughed.

"Bullshit. You've loved it since you were a kid. It's one of the best things about this town."

His friend snorted in agreement.

Will went on, "I wasn't kidding about Jordie being fucked up."

"You think he stopped taking his pills?"

Will didn't laugh. "Maybe," he said, nodding back toward the tent, which was now in the distance behind them. An old Puff Daddy song, its lyrics cleaned of numerous obscenities, could barely be heard.

Josh snorted again. They had reached Main Street and waited for traffic to clear in front of them, cars still pulling away from the end of the fireworks display, others trying to park to catch some of the music in the tent. It was a little colder than it had been, and Will suddenly shivered.

"Don't know about his meds," Josh answered, "but he's as big a weedhead as ever. I noticed him pull a pint bottle from his pants during his first set, too."

"That's part of what I'm talking about. When he's on his medication, Jordie's even tempered. Mild and funny as hell and wouldn't hurt a fly. Remember all that crazy stuff he used to do in grade school, just to make us laugh? And that time he flipped out when we found that puppy that had been hit by a car?"

"He cried like it had been his."

Will's face darkened, and he nodded his head. "And remember that time in seventh grade when he didn't take his pills, just to see what would happen?"

There was an opening in the traffic, and Josh dashed out into the street, Will after him. They reached the other side and began to walk quickly; Will checked his watch—it was within five to eleven.

"You bet your ass I remember," Will said, quickening his pace. "Tore up a classroom and almost killed old Peterson. They were going to throw him out—*shit*."

They had stopped abruptly in front of a convenience store with the name BURRITA'S over it; the lights within were out and the hours posted in the window stated that they closed at 7:00 on Sundays.

"I forgot what day it was," Will said. "We won't find anything open now."

"Just as well," Josh laughed; he had reached into his wallet and found it empty. "And I know you haven't got more than a buck on you," he continued, "you cheap bastard."

"Let's go back."

They reversed their steps, crossing to the other side of Main Street as soon as they could and walking along the park fence till they came to the entrance.

The tent glowed like a pumpkin from within, and they could see shadows of the dancers moving in strange shapes across the orange canvas surface.

"Looks cool," Josh said. He glanced at Will. "So spit it out. I can tell there's still something on your mind."

"It was just too normal in Jordie's house tonight. Everything looked like it had been cleaned, just for us. You know his mom and his aunt—"

"She ain't really his aunt, dude."

"That's just a rumor—"

"Jordie told me himself. It's why his father left. Jordie didn't seem to give a crap, one way or the other—"

"Well, anyway, I don't ever remember the house

228

being all that clean. Tonight it looked like it had been scrubbed. And when I asked him about the Halloween decorations in the windows, he laughed and said he put them there himself. Can you see Jordie taking the time to do something like that?"

Now Will laughed. "No way. He's a bigger slacker than you or me."

"There was just something weird in that house, is all."

"And why do you care?"

For the first time that evening Will looked at his friend in a completely sober way. "It's just that I think we should be responsible for our friends, is all. If we're not, why bother to have friends?"

Josh studied his face for a moment, then broke out in a grin. "Man, we've got to find you another beer!" he said. "You're *way* too serious!"

At midnight the last record was played, with Charlie Fredericks, one of the local sheriff's deputies, politely telling Jordie, with Josh and Will helping him by this time, that it was time to call it a night. Fredericks, who wasn't much older than Will, was a good guy and whispered to Will, "Tell your friend Jordie to leave the bottle home next time or I'll have to bust him. He's been acting strange all night, and, from what I hear, for the last week or so. I've already told him I'm gonna keep an eye on him." He slapped Will lightly on the back and walked away.

The music ended, the crowd left and they broke down the equipment in short order, pulling out cables, stacking the amp and turntables, slipping the vinyl LPs that littered the table and ground into their paper sleeves, their album covers, and then into the plastic milk crates that held them. Will and Josh carried the heavy speakers out first, hauling them by their handles and handing them into the bed of Josh's truck.

By twelve-thirty they were completely packed and on their way back to Jordie's house.

In the closed cab of the truck they could smell the overpowering alcohol odor of vodka on Jordie's breath.

"Say, Jordie, how much did you drink?" Josh asked, adding the deputy's warning.

"Fuck 'im," Jordie grinned, pulling an empty pint bottle from the deep leg pocket of his baggy pants and letting it fall to the floor. He giggled, pulling another empty pint from the other leg pocket, also empty. He frowned momentarily, then reached into his jacket pocket and produced a third bottle, three-quarters full. He unscrewed the top and took a pull.

"Jesus, you're gonna kill yourself drinking like that!" Josh said, and Will added, "Why don't you give me that."

Jordie turned to him, and for a moment there was a murderous rage in his eyes. Then he handed the pint to Will and grinned. "Plenty more where that came from."

Will slipped the pint into his own pocket. He asked quietly, "Are you still taking your pills, Jordie?"

"Just like on the list," Jordie answered, a bit slurrily. "Always follow the list."

"Isn't it a bad idea to drink so much while you're on your meds?"

Jordie swung his head around, and again that murderous glow came into his eyes. "Don't tell me what to do."

Tamping a touch of fear crawling up his back, Will kept his voice level. "I'm just thinking about you, bud—"

"Well, don't." He waved his hand, his anger gone. "Got a list . . ."

"What kind of list—"

"Here we are!" Josh interrupted, pulling with a braking squeal into Jordie's driveway. He pushed open his door and gave Will a look that said, "Not now."

They unloaded everything into the house, first setting up the folding table in Jordie's immaculately clean room and then arranging the amp and other equipment. The records came next, and while Will and Josh carried the last of the milk crates in, Jordie was meticulously lining up everything.

"Jeez," Josh said, trying to sound cheerful, "when did you learn to make a bed?"

Jordie looked up quickly. "It was on the list. I do everything that's on the list."

Will was about to open his mouth, but Josh shot him another look that told him to hold off.

"Guess we should get going," Josh said.

Jordie was inspecting his mixer, pushing it into line with the amp. He nodded without looking up.

"See you around," Josh added. "You said your mom and aunt will be back in a few days?"

231

Jordie nodded again, reaching into his still unzipped jacket to pull out yet another pint bottle of vodka, this one unopened. He twisted the metal cap off with a snap and swallowed some of it.

In the cab of Josh's truck, Will said, "Can I talk now?"

"You're right, he's completely fucked up," Josh said. "Every room looked like it had been scrubbed by a Navy swabbie. And he's drinking way too much. We have to keep an eye on him."

In his room, Jordie heard the roar of Josh's truck peeling out of his driveway and up the street. He was finished with the equipment, everything was lined up perfectly, just like the list said.

He pulled the list from his pocket, opening it carefully on a clear spot on his dj table, and smoothed it out. It was a long list now, and growing.

He fished a pen, which he now always carried with him, out of his pocket. He paused, as if listening to something only he could hear.

After consideration, he nodded, and added to the bottom of the list:

Kill Will and Josh.

CHAPTER THIRTY-SIX

Annabeth Turner stood before a large, heavy-looking wooden door painted a dark shade of orange. The door curved up into a half-circle at the top. Inset into this section was stained glass in the shape of a pumpkin. The glass had been stained the same color as the door. The stained glass section was too high to try to look into, so she rang the bell.

The house the door was attached to, which was at 1420 Acre Street, was a low, squatting, gloomy affair. Though it was just off Main Street, it looked as if it had shrunk away from the larger community of houses. It was surrounded by trees on all sides, which seemed to press in on it. Unraked leaves of dark golden red and brown and yellow had washed like ocean drifts against the foundation of the house, and a tall pine had fallen over, victim to some storm or fierce wind, and lay on the right side of the house, with its root system, now as dried as a knot of branches, pointing like an arrow at the front walk. Though it was daylight, and the last day of Pumpkin Days, with noise and laughter and bright October Saturday sunshine behind her on Main Street, Annabeth felt as if she had walked into a gloomy forest.

She rang the bell again, and this time heard a deep *bong, bong* echo far within the house.

There was the sound of shuffling, slippered feet approaching the door, which seemed to go on for much too long a time.

Finally they stopped, without seeming to get any louder.

She saw a shadow pass across the stained glass pumpkin.

The door made an unnaturally loud creaking sound as it opened a wide crack, giving her a view of an old wrinkled face, like the face of a capuchin monkey attached to a thin, robed body not much taller than her own.

"Yes?"

A shadow seemed to pass across the whole world; she glanced up and saw, through the dark treetops that a huge white cloud had crossed the sun.

The voice was strong and deep, but papery. The eyes, behind spectacles as thick as pats of butter, were large but rheumy, extremely light blue, a blue that was almost white. A tuft of long wispy white hair fell from high on his forehead back over the rear of his skull, which was almost orange.

"Are you T. R. Reynolds?" Annabeth asked in as strong a voice as she could muster.

The wizened monkey's head broke into a smile.

"You must have read my book," he said. "No one calls me T. R. but my publisher, who is me, of course."

The door opened wider and now Annabeth smelled Vicks Vapo Rub, and another, drier smell, like old books. Reynolds, she now saw, was indeed shod in slippers, which looked to be of old cracked black leather; there was golden piping around the foot opening. The visible portion of his foot between slipper and the bottom of his cuffed flannel pajamas was blue-veined and delicate-looking.

Annabeth thought that if she blew on the man he might break into dust motes.

"And you are?" Reynolds asked, his voice still showing pleasure; he had thankfully stopped grinning, which had showed her a mouth of dentures backed by few other teeth and red inflamed gums.

"My name is Annabeth Turner," she answered in the serious voice she had practiced all morning. "Yes, I read your book and loved it. I'd like to talk to you about volume two—"

"Ah!" Reynolds said, in a stronger, suddenly sad voice. "In that case, you'll have to come in. . . ."

The door opened wider, making an even louder creak, which Annabeth was sure would bring someone running from Main Street. But as she stepped into the now wide opening, the outside world, sounds and light, seemed chopped off as if with an axe.

The door closed behind her, leaving her in almost total darkness except for a faint amber cast through the pumpkin stained glass in the door.

By its light she saw a low wooden stool behind the

door, against the wall—Reynolds must have used it to step up and look out at her through the pumpkin window.

Reynolds was already shuffling off down a hallway. His slippers made a much larger, more annoying sound here inside the house. As he passed a doorway he flicked a switch on the hallway wall and a flare of illumination burst within a room through the opening. Now Annabeth could make out art objects in the hallway—a dark wooden chest in the shape of a squatting beast, with its head hinged open at the cranium to reveal a red felt-lined cavity within; dark paintings on the walls, mostly forest scenes; a sconce in the shape of a pumpkin without a top, unlit.

"Come into the parlor, Ms. Turner!" Reynolds rasped heartily. She caught up to him only to see him disappear into the back of a room even gloomier than the hallway—deeply dark red damask chairs and, behind an ebony coffee table, a Sheridan sofa that almost looked to be upholstered in black velvet. The only illumination in the room came from a single lamp next to one of the damask chairs, which she quickly sat down in.

Reynolds was fussing over a dark fireplace against the far wall, leaning down and poking at it with a long twig; she realized he was trying to light a fire within with a long match. The mantle above the fireplace was lined with what looked like tiny taxidermied animals—a field mouse, a chipmunk, a red squirrel in a fiendish pose, on its hind legs with its front claws ready for a fight, mouth opened in a silent hiss.

Reynolds threw the match down in disgust and turned around. "Is it all right if we don't have a fire, Ms. Turner?"

"It's warm enough in here," Annabeth answered.

It was—it was as dry and airless as the inside of a toaster.

"Very well." He shuffled to the black sofa and settled himself in the middle of it. It seemed to swallow him up for a moment; then he came to rest and sat with his hands folded.

"What, then, would you like to know about volume two of my book?"

Annabeth replied, "Will it be out soon?"

There was a long moment of silence, during which Annabeth heard the whisper of a ticking clock somewhere else, faraway in the depths of the house.

"It will never be out," T.R. Reynolds finally replied.

"Why not?"

The pause was longer this time; Annabeth distinctly heard the faraway striking of a chime for four o'clock.

"Because I want to live."

Annabeth was about to speak when Reynolds spoke again. "You see, Ms. Turner, the legend about Samhaim is true."

"I know. I've . . . spoken to him."

"So have I, Ms. Turner." His eyes behind his spectacles seemed to have faded entirely to white. "In a pumpkin field, last October, he appeared to me and asked me politely—a voice in my head, not unkind, but with what I would call an undercurrent of authority—not to publish the second volume of my book. At that time I had finished writing it, and had only to satisfy my own curiosity regarding the existence of Samhain. He had no problem with the first volume, he even complimented me on it, but did not want the second part to be published. 'A special request,' he called it."

He leaned closer, looking slightly to the side of where Annabeth was sitting, before focusing on her again. "I don't see very well these days, I'm afraid. And my health, as you can see, is precarious. However . . ."

He rose from the black couch unsteadily, and shuffled off to a large chest on the wall behind him. Above the chest was yet another dark painting of a landscape: a tiny house, lit from within, surrounded by mountains and a brooding sky.

He drew the top drawer of the chest open. It slid out with the screech of dried wood. He took something out, long and bulky, and shuffled back to the sofa. He placed what he held—a large, thick dun-colored folder—on the ebony coffee table.

He sat back, the sofa swallowing even more of him.

"There it is, Ms. Turner. He told me to give it to you when you came."

Annabeth sat stunned, and then reached for the folder, drawing it into her lap.

Reynolds was studying her closely. "The thing I don't understand—one of many things, I'm afraid—

is why he chose you instead of me. But he became quite peevish when I asked that question."

Annabeth said nothing.

"*Quite* peevish. You might study the copyright page on this second volume, Ms. Turner. It will prove instructive. And I won't counsel you to be careful, because you already haven't been. Perhaps someday my son, who is in California with his mother at the moment, will return and continue my work. Do show yourself out."

As Annabeth got up, clutching the folder, she again smelled the odor of Vicks, and saw that T. R. Reynolds was crying. She stood watching him. He turned his wizened face away from her and lifted his paper thin, blue-veined hands to cover his face.

"Please go."

She quickly left the room, the hallway, the house, hearing the monstrously loud creak of the front door slamming behind her.

On the street, as if a switch had been thrown, the day was still bright, blue-skied, chilly-warm with early autumn. She looked back, and the Reynolds house looked even darker, lost in its night of trees.

She hurried home, enjoying the late warmth of the day.

Back in her room, sitting at her desk, she drew out the mass of paper, which had already been printed in proof pages, awaiting only corrections and return to the printer. She turned quickly past the title page, feeling a thrill at the words *Volume Two, 1941–the present*, and scanned the copyright page. It looked similar to that of the first volume: date of (proposed) publication, ISBN number, copyright information, author information for library cataloging purposes . . .

Her eyes locked on the author information, which she had, indeed, looked over in the first volume, but which had not come back to strike her as odd until today.

The date of birth for T. R. Reynolds was listed, making him only twenty-eight years old.

CHAPTER THIRTY-SEVEN

"I still have my doubts."

The girl will be fine. The two men I am already sure of, replied Samhain.

"I've told you before, this way is the trickiest. There are other ways."

But none as direct.

"You've failed with this before—"

Nineteen forty-one was an experiment. I learned from it.

"And 1981?"

A failure, I admit. But I learned from that, too. It is the unpredictability of these creatures that astounds me. It always has. You assume you know them—

"One would think that Death would know them well."

One would think that the opposite of creation would know them better, Dark One. Death is only part of what they are. Sometimes they almost interest me. That Grant almost interests me.

"As long as you say 'almost.' What I found interesting was the way you moved him aside. When these humans truly start to interest you I will wonder about you. It is still the girl I have questions about."

As I said, she will be fine. All will be fine. And, as I said, we have insurance. My time of the year is coming, and all will be ready.

"I hope so, my friend. For your sake."

CHAPTER THIRTY-EIGHT

The Pumpkin Tender was desolate.

It had begun to rain the day after the end of Pumpkin Days, and it continued to rain for four days after that. Cold, damp rain, the precursor to winter snow, a slate gray sky, the ground sodden with water. His fields, empty as they were, had gone quickly to ruin, furrows filling with mud, some turning to sodden shallow lakes of brown water. The pumpkins in his special field had begun to rot; normally he would have built a shelter for them, tended them until well past Thanksgiving, ensuring that the few that remained planted in the ground were nourished, their stalks bright green as long as possible before the coming winter. Now they lay, picked and unpicked alike, in a slurry mess, the ripest of them rotting from within, bursting along their seems, ruined, smelling of decay.

For three days he had waited for the large pumpkin with two lobes to speak to him again, huddled beneath his wet blanket, shivering, eyes glued to the fruit—but nothing had happened. Finally, when he ventured close enough to inspect it, he saw that its stem had dropped away from its top and worms were crawling into the soggy opening, feasting on the grayish-yellow pulp within.

After that he moved farther away from his fields, limping up into the low hills surrounding Orange-field, where no one could find him.

There was a cave set into one of the hills, and he spent one night in it, but then what looked like a wolf, but might have been a feral dog, chased him out, teeth bared, growling. After that there was nowhere completely dry for him to stay, and after a second night under the rain his skin was wrinkled as a prune and splotched purple.

He was afraid of his own dreams, and slept little.

He ate nothing for the first day, but then, his stomach screaming with hunger, he foraged for roots and whatever else looked edible on the second. In doing this he made one great mistake, and spent an entire night groaning in a squat, his sodden pants around his ankles as his bowels sought to tear themselves from his body.

The next morning he awoke after barely an hour of sleep, shivering and with a fever. His leg ached like fire.

It was then that the wolf, or feral dog, tracked him and began to circle as he lay on the ground. He prayed that the beast might attack him and tear out his throat and be done with it. Everything would be over then. All the dreams, the bad memories, the shattered bits of his life, everything he didn't want put together again.

He actually fell asleep, in the rain, and waited, almost soothed, for the worst.

But nothing happened, and when he woke up the rain had stopped and the cold clouds were pulling away. Behind them was a measure of blue sky, and then the sun came back and the temperature rose.

He was almost dry, covered in his Army blanket, which had, miraculously, become dry itself. He no longer trembled and his fever was gone.

His leg was free of pain.

He sat up on dry ground, on a little rise that fell away to dry woods in front and in back of him.

The dog that had followed him was a few yards away, torn to shreds, its own throat ripped apart, its mouth open, teeth bared, in a silent cry of agony.

The Pumpkin Tender began to rock back and forth, making weeping sounds.

There, there, the voice in his head came, *didn't I tell you everything would be all right?*

His rocking became more frantic, his mewling sounds more frightened.

The thing in the black cape melted out of the woods in front of him. In sunlight, there was still no face visible, only a dark, shaped void beneath the cowl. There was no physical form visible beneath the folds of the garment—it was as if the garment itself were the creature.

Aaron, the thing said in a soothing voice, *if I'd known you'd be so upset by what I told you, I never would have said it. Do you think I want to hurt you? I only want to help you. I thought remembering would help you.*

The Pumpkin Tender continued to rock, shaking his head violently.

Do you believe I want to help you?

Again Aaron shook his head violently.

How can I prove it to you? Would you like to forget again?

Now the Pumpkin Tender nodded, making a choking noise. He tried closing his eyes, but the image of the caped thing was still there, as if his lids didn't exist. He made a louder choked crying sound.

The shape advanced on him. Suddenly it put its hand—a pale white, shapeless thing—on Aaron's head. It was colder than ice. A feeling more numbing than any he had ever felt went down through Aaron's head along his back, spreading like expanding cracks in a frozen pond.

I can let you forget again, Aaron, the shape whispered. *I can take the memories away from you.*

Frantically, he nodded, in fear and need.

But tell me first—do the memories hurt you?

A quick nod.

Do they make you want to hurt yourself?

Another nod.

Do they?

He cried out, yanking his head away from the creature's touch, and fell shivering to the ground. Over and over he mouthed in silent agony the word, "Yes."

246

Good, then. Remember them one more time, and then I will take them from you. . . .

The creature's hand reached out, impossibly long, and its hand once more rested on the Pumpkin Tender's head. . . .

He wasn't the Pumpkin Tender, or Frankenstein. He was Aaron Peters, Private First Class, and he had a letter in his pocket from his sweetheart. Peggy hadn't written in a week, and he was afraid the mail had been held up or censored out of existence, or maybe in the crashed C-47 cargo plane that had gone down ten days before after being hit by a rebel rocket.

But now he finally had a letter from her in his breast pocket, next to his heart, and the world was right again.

"Hey, dogshit, you gonna read that thing or what?" Kip Berger kidded him. They had started out on a reconnaissance sweep an hour ago, the two of them on the ground with a truck fifty yards behind, just after chow and just after mail call, which had come at the last minute.

Aaron grinned and patted his heart. "Got it right here, numb-nuts. I always put her letters here before I do the day's work. Keeps me safe."

"She must be one helluva bang."

Aaron's grin disappeared and he turned to Berger, balling his fists. "I'd take that back—"

But Berger's big smile calmed him down. "I'm just jealous, is all. I've been married to my fist so long, it makes me crazy when I see a guy with a real girl waiting for him."

Aaron relaxed. For the next five minutes they walked on silently, inspecting the bushes in front of them, the dry horizon ahead of them.

Finally Berger, who couldn't be quiet for long, said, "I hate this job. The shitheels with the minesweepers go through ahead of us, and then we get to hope they did their fucking job and cleared out all the fragmentation stake mines, the claymores—"

"You know how it is—some of these bastards are homemade, or minimum metal jobs, and don't have enough metal parts for the clearance robots or detectors to pick them up. You can thank the Russians for selling some of them to these warlord assholes."

"Yeah, well, I still think it sucks—" Suddenly Berger stopped dead. His face went white. "Hey, Aaron . . ."

Aaron stood still, and looked to where Berger was pointing: at his right boot, frozen in place.

Berger said in a measured voice, "I think I stepped on one of the fuckers we just talked about, bud."

"Don't move."

"No shit."

Aaron studied the ground around Berger's boot, looking for another slight depression or suspicious turn in the soil.

"Looks like there's only one," Aaron said. "No trip wire, or your leg would be gone by now. It's a wooden plate. It'll go off if you lift your foot."

"That's the good news, right?"

"There's only good news today, Kip."

"Tell it to the Marines. My foot is starting to fall asleep."

"Just hang on, pal."

Berger managed a faint smile, and pointed to his crotch. "Hang onto this."

"I'll get the C.O."

"Well, hurry it up, then!" Berger's voice had taken on a note of urgency.

Aaron quickly covered the ground they had cleared, breaking into a trot. The C.O.'s truck was stopped fifty yards back, and he reached it, saluted and reported what had happened.

"Shit," the C.O., a small, swarthy man with a two-day stubble and tired eyes, said. "It sounds home-made, and it's probably got a big charge in it. Last time we tried to move a weight over one of those mines to transfer the pressure, it still blew. Cut the poor bastard in half."

"Is there something else we can do?"

The C.O. shook his head. "S.O.P., Peters, which means they haven't come up with anything better. I know they tried just about everything else you could think of—foam, debris containment, you name it. Weight transfer is still the only thing that might work."

He gave an order, and the sergeant sitting next to him jumped out and went to the back of the truck. Aaron followed him.

"How much does Berger weigh?" the Sergeant asked.

"I'd say about one-seventy. Maybe one-seventy-five."

The sergeant pulled a box out and began to fill it with measured weights. "That means we need about sixty pounds. You think you can handle this alone?"

"Sure."

The sergeant finished with the box, closed and latched it and handed it to Peters, along with three five-foot sections of metal pole. He explained exactly what had to be done.

"Tell the poor bastard we're praying for him."

"Right."

Aaron lugged the box back to Berger and set it on the ground with a grunt.

"You weigh about one-seventy, right?"

"One eighty-five."

"Shit."

Berger looked at him, the strain evident on his features. "Whatever you've got in the box, use it. I can't wait too much longer. There are pins and needles up and down my leg, and I can't feel it anymore."

"Fine." Aaron shuffled the box along the ground toward Berger's frozen foot, stopping about six inches away.

"You ready?"

"No."

"What's the matter?"

Berger looked at him with frightened eyes. "What the hell do you mean, *what's the matter*? I'm scared shitless! And don't tell me this works every time, because I know it hardly ever works. I was at the same briefing you were. I was sitting right next to you when they said 'Say good-bye to your ass' if you get in this jam."

To his embarrassment, Aaron noticed that Berger had peed himself.

"Maybe they were wrong." Aaron was fitting the first section of the pole to a catch on the box; then he would fit subsequent sections into the rear of the one in front of it, until he was fifteen feet away. Then he would push the box forward to replace Berger's weight on the mine. "You set?"

"Not yet, bud. I want you to do me a big favor."

Peters snapped the last section of pole into place. He looked up quizzically.

Berger said, "I want you to read me that letter from your girl."

Aaron straightened. "Jeez."

Berger pleaded, "Please, bud. For luck. Maybe some of the luck you always get will fall on me."

"You got it." Aaron put down the pole and pulled the letter out from its place near his heart. He ripped open one edge and pulled the single sheet out, waiting for the whiff of perfume that always accompanied Peggy's letters to him.

There was no perfume.

He flipped open the letter.

"Read it," Berger demanded. "Out loud."

Aaron was scanning the letter, his eyes starting at the signature on the bottom—which read *Yours sincerely,* instead of *All my love*—to the top, which started: *Dear Aaron, Things have happened in the last few weeks* . . .

"Read it, dammit!" Berger begged.

The world drew away from Aaron Peters; suddenly he didn't see the dusty road, or Berger, or the thin blue sky of Mogadishu, or anything. A hissing came into his head, and the spot next to his heart where the letter had been began to burn as if it were on fire. His hand holding the letter dropped to his side, and the words *no longer*, and *wish you well in the future* drained out of him as if a stopcock had been opened on his life. He was suddenly dry, and light as air. The letter floated to earth. He was standing next to Berger but didn't see him or hear his shouting voice.

Then suddenly he did. *"What the hell?"* he heard as he put his hands on Berger and pushed, and slid his boots forward to replace himself on the mine, which then went off.

He heard the explosion from far away, and saw Berger cut into parts in front of him, as if drawn and quartered in midair—his legs and thighs, suddenly red, flying one way while the top parts, bloody as well, a severed arm, the rest of the torso, with something heaving in the open chest and with the other arm still reaching for him and the face still asking *"What the hell?"* flew impossibly far the other way. And then as Berger receded everything faded from his face, all emotion and questions, and he turned white and dead. And then there was a burn up Aaron's own leg and sound came back in a rush like a turned-up volume knob and he heard that tearing sound, of meat being ripped off a bone, his own meat and Berger's, and then another louder sound of all the screams, his own impossibly high screams until something slammed into his chin and up through his mouth. . . .

* * *

The impossibly cold hand on the Pumpkin Tender's head slid away in a retreating caress.

Suddenly the memories were gone.

All of them, as if a switch had clicked off the lights in his head.

He was the Pumpkin Tender, and Frankenstein.

He was no longer Aaron Peters, Private First Class, who had murdered his buddy and tried, unsuccessfully, to murder himself.

He was nothing now, only a mess of a former man—a man who remembered little, if anything, and took care of pumpkins.

Didn't I tell you I'd take care of you? Haven't I always taken care of you?

The touch of the freezing hand came back, and with it one more memory, which flared briefly in his head before dissipating like smoke:

When he came back from Somalia, and after all the time in the VA hospital, and then the discharge, an honorable one because the administration didn't want any more blots on the Somalia campaign, especially not after losing all those men when they went after that warlord—after all that time, there was nothing wrong with his memory. He could remember what he had done perfectly well. He had begun to limp around Orangefield, keeping his horrible secret to himself, from his family, from his friends, because he couldn't live with it.

And then he decided not to live with it.

So one night the first October after he returned,

when the moon looked Halloween-orange as it rose off the horizon, and it was cold, he had gone out to one of the empty pumpkin fields on the outskirts of Orangefield, a field owned by a man named Froelich, and he had stood in that almost empty, almost picked-clean pumpkin field, smelling rotting sweet pumpkin carcasses around him and facing the moon, and he put his service revolver to his head.

Only something had risen out of that field in front of him, something like a black cape, which blotted the moon from view, and he had lowered the service revolver while the thing made promises.

You already belong to me, the thing said, reasonably. *You should have died in Somalia, the way you intended, so you are already mine. You're living on borrowed time, and in agony, but I will protect you. I will make you forget. Isn't forgetfulness what you really want, Aaron? Isn't that why you came out here tonight—to forget?*

He nodded, dropping the gun. He began to weep, and tried to talk with his ruined mouth: "I . . . k-k-killed—"

Yes, Aaron. But I'll help you to forget, until it's time for you to help me. Do you understand?

Aaron was weeping. "I . . . ki . . . illed . . ."

And then the freezing had first fallen on his head, and with it blessed forgetfulness.

And then, suddenly, he understood what he could do, what loving service he could perform, and he had become, then and now, the Pumpkin Tender.

CHAPTER THIRTY-NINE

Kathy Marks could not stop thinking about Annabeth Turner.

What is it about her?

Ever since Annabeth had taken three restricted books from the library—returning them the next day while Kathy was not on duty, which the librarian was sure had been deliberate—Kathy had felt a strange affinity for the girl, something that went beyond the tug of outsider recognition she had felt for Annabeth initially.

Is it because she lost her father, and I lost my parents?

A brief memory of Aunt Jane and Uncle Ed, who'd taken Kathy in after the car accident, rose into her consciousness, and she shivered.

Or am I afraid for her because of what happened to me afterward?

Annabeth and her mother had moved to Orange-field, the librarian knew, at the beginning of the summer. Mr. Turner had died the year before. Kathy had deduced that things were not good at home, that Annabeth's mother, in the girl's phrase, had "problems." There had also been the hint of social services involvement, which could mean anything from child neglect to outright abuse. Kathy had driven by the house one evening after work and found it unkept and lonely looking—the poor relation on a block of neatly trimmed cape houses.

Why am I so worried about her?

Without really knowing why, she suddenly decided that tonight she would stop by the house and see the girl.

There was something sad and desperate about her, something that reminded her of herself at that age.

And something else that she couldn't put her finger on, something to do with the voice she had heard in the library that night. . . .

The library was busy for a Tuesday night, and she was occupied until just before nine o'clock. And then, suddenly, she was alone. Her student assistant, Paul, after turning out most of the lights, was through the door at the stroke of the hour, and with the bang of the closing, locked door, Kathy found herself with a little paperwork and a silent library.

The wind had picked up, making that sound against the windows that always reminded her of moaning.

And now there was another sound that drowned out the moan.

It was the voice she had heard the night Annabeth had taken the three restricted books.

Kathy.

Again, as it had that night, the vaguest of dark memories tried to rise, then melted away. She felt herself go cold all over.

Kathy. Speak to me.

The voice had moved to one of the other windows, and then she heard it from the darkened back of the library.

Kathy.

She heard the shuffle of steps in one of the aisles, the sound of books being moved aside.

Call me Sam . . .

The librarian marched to the bank of lights by the front door, threw on the fluorescents in the back of the library.

She felt something cold touch her finger, brush up her left arm and across her neck. There was a whisper in her ear.

It's me. Samhain . . .

The windows began to rattle—all of them at once, a sound as if they would all shatter to bits. The suspended overhead fluorescent lights began to sway.

Kathy ran to her desk, grabbed for her purse and jacket.

A stack of books, waiting to be checked in, flew off the desk in three directions.

Kathy.

She ran for the door and the newspaper rack came alive as she passed, magazines and the daily newspapers flying up like birds flapping at her.

She covered her face and cried out as newspapers hit her in the face, magazines slapped at her legs.

Annabeth is mine.

The voice was all around her, whispering in her ear and shouting at her from the back of the library simultaneously.

The window rattling rose to the breaking point—

And then stopped.

The library was silent.

The overhead hanging lights swayed to a squeaking halt.

The newspapers fluttered to the floor around her.

Kathy Marks stood by the doorway, panting, eyes wide.

She let out a single, frightened sob.

In her car, she regained her composure. She sat steadying her breath, watching the darkened library building in front of her. The lights were out, the building quiet.

Whoever you are, she thought, *you won't stop me.*

As she pulled away, once more determined to visit Annabeth Turner, the lights in the library, unseen to her, blinked on for a moment, and something dark passed before the front windows.

The house was even untidier and sadder looking than she remembered. There were empty garbage cans at the curb that needed taking in; the grass needed mowing; the flower beds to either side of the front door were choked with dry weeds; the paint on the shutters was peeling, and the front steps groaned with rotted wood when she stepped on them.

She rang the doorbell three times, hearing nothing, and then knocked loudly on the door. She still heard nothing.

Daring herself, she walked around to the side of the house, almost stepping on a rusted rake carelessly left tines up.

The first floor windows along the front were all dark, but she detected the glow of faint light in a window on the second floor of the house.

She walked to the back of the house, which was even more overgrown, and looked up—there was a light on in the single second-story window.

She went back to the front door and banged on it repeatedly. She heard the rustle of movement inside the house, followed by a grunt. She banged again. She heard more movement, a slurred voice: "Whozzit?"

"Mrs. Turner," she called, "it's Kathy Marks, from the Orangefield Library. May I speak with you, please?"

There was a groan, and then silence.

Kathy banged on the door again. "Mrs. Turner, I need to talk with you about Annabeth!"

Another groan from within, and then a sound as if someone were falling to the floor. She heard a curse, and then slow, measured steps from behind the door.

The door was yanked open, and a blowsy, angry face appeared.

"What the hell you want?"

The door was thrown all the way open, and the woman, who was dressed in a dirty housecoat and slippers, nearly lurched at her. The librarian was forced to step back by the strong sour smell of gin. Behind her the house was filthy, cluttered and dark, all the way back to the second-story stairway and the kitchen beyond, where a cat crouched, staring at her suspiciously.

"Mrs. Turner—"

"I said what the hell you want! Botherin' me at all hours! What'd she do? What'd the brat do?"

Kathy took a breath before answering reasonably: "Annabeth didn't do anything, Mrs. Turner. I'm here because I'm concerned about her—"

"Concerned about wha'? Get out! Leave me alone! I ain't a bad parent. I can do what has to be done! No goddamn social services bitch is gonna tell me otherwise!"

"I'm not from social services, Mrs. Turner—"

"Dammit! Leave us alone! Leave us all alone!"

Behind Mrs. Turner, Kathy saw Annabeth slowly descending the stairs and staring at her intently. She stopped at the bottom.

The librarian took a step forward and tried to reason directly with the girl. "Annabeth, can I speak with you please?"

"I brought the books back," the girl said defensively.

"It's not about that—"

Mrs. Turner suddenly lunged forward, holding on to Kathy Marks and breathing directly in her face. Kathy saw Annabeth run back up the stairs.

"It ain't right! Get out! Get out!"

Kathy moved back, disengaging herself from Mrs. Turner.

"I'm sorry I bothered you, Mrs. Turner."

"An' don't come back!" Mrs. Turner shouted, slamming the door shut.

The librarian stood staring at the front door for a moment.

I told you, she's mine.

It was the voice again, from the library.

Annabeth belongs to me, Kathy.

A swirl of pure cold rose up around her, like a tornado, driving her from the front walk.

Mine.

Kathy Marks turned and ran for her car, opening the door and slamming it behind her. The dervish of wind was left in the street, where it circled down to nothingness.

Kathy Marks drove slowly away, stopping once, without really knowing why, still breathing hard and trembling, to look back at the second floor of the house.

CHAPTER FORTY

"Dude!"

As Josh got out of the cab of his black Ford truck, Jordie nearly rushed forward to hug him. Josh took a step back, hesitating, but Jordie seemed to be in such a good mood that he gave a short laugh and allowed himself to be nearly picked up off the ground.

Jordie dropped him, looked around him into the truck's cab.

"Hey, were's Will?"

"Couldn't come," Josh answered. "Had to do some stuff for his mom."

"Mom. Yeah, cool."

Josh looked into his friend's face and saw that the pupils were wide as dimes.

Shit, hammered again, he thought.

"Maybe I should come back later, Jordie," he said.

He hitched a thumb at the cab. "Truck needs an oil change—"

"Hell, I'll *buy* you an oil change, after we move that shit I told you about. We'll go over to the Jiffy Lube, then pick up Will—"

"I don't think Will can make it at all today," Josh said.

"No shit?" A dark cloud passed over Jordie's face, and Josh thought he heard him mumble, "Not on the list, man . . ."

"List?"

Jordie seemed to touch earth again. "Shit, man— just you and me, then! Dynamic duo. Just like fifth grade!"

Josh was suddenly uncomfortable. He looked past Jordie at the house. The rest of the driveway was un-cluttered by cars, and the open garage was empty. "Your mom and aunt ever get home?"

"Huh? Sure! Days ago. They went out for lunch or something. You know how these modern couples are. . . ." He laughed, and leaned closer. "Hey, wanna get stoned?" he whispered.

The inside of the house looked as spotless as the last time he'd been in it. In fact, it looked *exactly* like the last time he'd been in it, more than a week and a half ago. There wasn't even a cereal box out of place in the kitchen. More out of curiosity than hunger, he opened the refrigerator and said, "Got anything to e—"

The fridge was completely empty, not even an egg in its plastic nest—no milk, no butter, no fruit in their bins, no cottage cheese . . .

A weird chill went up Josh's back.

"Jeez, Jordie, what the hell have you been living on?"

When he turned around Jordie was right in front of him, grinning as he pushed something long and brightly metallic into Josh's stomach.

"Sorry, man," Jordie whispered, "but it's on the list."

Josh opened his mouth wide to speak, but Jordie shook his head and ripped the blade viciously up through his middle.

A bright blurt of blood formed in Josh's open mouth, and then his eyes clouded over and he became a weight against the open refrigerator, which began to hum.

Jordie let him down easily to the floor, then pushed him aside with his booted foot and closed the refrigerator door.

"Have to clean that again, man," he said, focusing on the drops of red splattered on the door.

Find Will, the voice in his head told him.

Forty minutes later, after bringing Josh's body to the cellar and lining it up neatly with that of his mother and aunt, which were already limed and tarped, he climbed into the cab of Josh's truck and pulled it out onto the road. The day was bone chilly, but he wore only his light jacket over a T-shirt and jeans. In the flatbed was his dj equipment, carefully wrapped and tied down. On the seat next to him in the cab was an open piece of paper with Will's name on it and a pile of pill bottles. On the bottom of the list, after Will's name, was the phrase, *Take your meds, in the proportions I told you.*

Will's house was empty, which started to panic him, but the voice in his head calmed him down, telling him to take one Zyprexa, which he did dry, because he had forgotten to bring any vodka with him.

I didn't want you to bring any vodka, the voice said, and he said out loud, "Oh, yeah," and remembered one of the other things on the list.

And drive slowly, the voice added.

He slowed the truck down to thirty as he came into town, matching the speed limit.

It was a busy Thursday afternoon, and the business district of Orangefield was crowded with traffic. Most of the parking spots along Main were taken, and the bank parking lot was full. He spotted Will's mother's Malibu in one of the bank slots near the front.

Park across the street.

He circled around the block again, coming back out on Main Street behind the bank, and pulled into a street spot across from the bank as someone pulled out ahead of him.

Check the meter.

He got out of the car and saw that there were twenty minutes left on the parking meter.

Put a quarter in.

He started to protest, then stopped when a woman walking a baby stroller looked at him oddly.

Do it.

He fished a quarter out of his pocket, noting that it was a Delaware commemorative—hadn't his aunt collected those? Did she have this one? Maybe he should save it for her . . . and then remembered that she was dead and didn't collect them anymore. He slid the quarter into the meter slot.

Get back in the cab and wait for them to come out. Then follow them.

He did so, and turned on the radio; he turned the dial away from Josh's alternative rock station and zeroed in on the rap station he listened to. He cranked up the volume—

Turn it down.

"But—"

The voice was less pleasant: *Now.*

He shrugged and turned down the volume so that it couldn't be heard on the street.

After a half hour of music mixed with what seemed like a hundred commercials (*Got to find another station to listen to*, he thought) he was reaching for the dial when the voice said: *Look.*

He looked up and saw Will and his mother, a petite brunette with a no-nonsense look on her face, leaving the bank and heading for their car.

Follow.

Jordie turned on the engine and pulled out behind Will's car.

Back a little. So they don't see you.

He let another car pull out from the curb in front of him and kept himself a discrete distance behind that.

There were two more stops—the pharmacy, which Will's mother ran into while Will stayed behind the wheel, and then the supermarket.

Jordie groaned as Will and his mother parked and headed into the food store with a cart.

Be patient. Listen to the radio again. Take a Clozaril.

Jordie kept the radio on while he rummaged through the pile of pill bottles, drawing one oblong pill out and again swallowing it dry.

"Damn! I do need some vodka for that!" His eyes went to the liquor store next to the supermarket, but the voice said: *No.*

Anger flared up, but the pill kicked in quickly, calming him. He lazily spun the tuner on the radio, looking for a more commercial-free rap station, but it wasn't to be found.

"How long are we going to have to—"

There. They're coming out. Follow them like before.

"James Bond," Jordie laughed, bringing the truck's engine to life again.

He kept a distance from Will's car, and was rewarded when it headed straight out of town.

In a few minutes it had pulled off the main road into Will's neighborhood and then into his driveway, which sided a neat red ranch house with a small porch guarding the white front door.

Wait till they go in the house. Then follow them in and do it.

Jordie held back, parking on the street a few houses away while Will and his mother unloaded the groceries; as Will slammed the car's trunk closed and headed for the front door, Jordie pulled up and parked in front of Will's house. As he parked he rummaged beneath the mountain of pill bottles and found the knife he had used on Josh. It still had blood on it.

Get out. Do it.

Jordie climbed out of the truck's cab, hiding the knife in his jacket pocket; he felt something else in there, a bag with some of his marijuana in it.

"Man, sure could use a toke or two now—"

Do it.

He skipped up onto the porch like he had a thousand times, stepped to the side of the huge pumpkin there and reached for the doorbell.

He pushed the buzzer twice. As the door opened, revealing Will's surprised mother, a hand clamped on Jordie's arm from behind him as Jordie pulled the knife from his pocket, followed by the bag of marijuana, which fell to the ground.

Jordie twisted around to see the face of Deputy Sheriff Charlie Fredericks.

"*Jeez*," Fredericks said, tightening his grip on the hand with the knife in it. As he did so the knife fell to the ground. "I told you I'd keep an eye on you, Jordie—all I wanted to do was see if you were drunk or stoned!" He yanked both of Jordie's arms behind him while he fished out his cuffs and secured them.

He turned Jordie around. "What the hell were you up to?"

Jordie waited for the voice to give him instructions, tell him what to do or say, but the voice was gone.

He looked the deputy sheriff in the face and grinned. "I was just gonna kill 'em, is all. Just like the others at my house."

PART V

HALLOWEEN

CHAPTER FORTY-ONE

The banner had been taken down over City Hall, and the tent was gone from Rainier Park. The grandstand had been dismantled along Main Street. There were no more fireworks or pumpkin pie eating contests or parades or pumpkin rolling contests or music. The votes for Pumpkin Queen had been tallied, the winner crowned and feted and sent home.

Pumpkin Days were long over.

But the orange-painted stripe down the middle of Main Street remained, and so did the lights and the decorations and, of course, the pumpkins.

There was still the matter of Halloween.

October 31st dawned damp and cold, but by nine in the morning the misty rain had dissipated and blue sky broke through. By eleven the sun had dried the leaves to crisp colors, and the world smelled of apples and burning woodsmoke and candles and pumpkin innards.

As if by magic, the pumpkins of Orangefield, which had gone to bed the night before as faceless fruit, had reappeared in the morning as guardians and monsters. Not real monsters but carved ones, with distinct faces—evil or friendly grins, toothless or toothsome, some with ears, some with triangles for noses, or circles, or rough diamond shapes or no noses at all. There was the work of artists and the work of amateurs and tots.

Orangefield was overpopulated by a race of orange faces.

The sun got high but never hot. As the day wore on the sky became bluer, colder, and the wind, a Halloween wind, began to whip the leaves into leaf tornados and whistle through the pumpkins and make them sing. The store shelves were empty of candy. It was Friday, and after the schools let out for the week there was much unboxing and pinning and cutting as costumes were unpacked or made, sheets instantly became ghosts, children grew wax fangs or became suddenly vampires or bats or space invaders. The children of Orangefield disappeared, replaced by one-of-everything-monsters, waiting for dark.

In the Orangefield Library, Kathy Marks thought of nothing but Annabeth Turner. There was a place in her that turned to ice whenever the image of the tall young girl rose into her mind, and there were roiling memories that tried again and again to climb up from Kathy's forgotten past but refused to become real.

She was sure the girl was in some sort of danger.

She had hoped Annabeth would return to the library to talk to her, but it hadn't happened. Kathy had even stopped by the girl's house again, but this time no one had come to the door. The librarian had taken to calling the house on the telephone at intervals over the last few days, but to no avail.

For the fourth time that day, she called Annabeth's house, but there was still no answer.

Outside, the wind moaned across the windows. The streets were beginning to fill up with costumed trick-or-treaters. Soon the trickle would turn into a torrent.

At five o'clock, in a half hour, Kathy would close the library early for the holiday. She had already turned away a few hopeful costumed children, explaining patiently that it was library policy not to serve candy, and that she would be happy to accommodate them when they visited her house later.

Stroking her left forearm lightly with her fingers, she stared at the clock and then reached once more for the phone.

CHAPTER FORTY-TWO

Annabeth sat up, blinked and said, "What day is it?"

Don't you know, Wizard? It's our day. It's Halloween.

Halloween? Could it really be Halloween?

Yes, Wizard, the voice said, soothing. *Finally. The day I show you what I promised. After you do one thing for me.*

Annabeth stretched, sat up in her desk chair. It felt as if she had been sitting for days. She probably had been. She knew she had stopped going to school, hadn't eaten much lately and couldn't remember the last time she'd bathed. She looked down at herself and couldn't remember the last time she had changed her clothes, either.

But none of that matters, Wizard. What matters is that you'll see where your father is.

"Yes," she said, and suddenly the strange feelings melted away, replaced by a kind of peace. "I'll see where my father is."

She looked down at the open manuscript pages on her desk, the proof pages of T. R. Reynolds's *Occult Practices in Orangefield and Chicawa County, New York, Volume Two*. The pages she had last turned to were crumpled and stained—she had fallen asleep on them.

But they seemed to glow with truth.

The phone next to her bed rang—she seemed to remember it ringing on and off for some time. She pushed herself away from the desk and reached to answer it.

Don't.

Her hand froze above the phone, and it suddenly stopped ringing.

Almost immediately it began to ring again, and without thinking she snatched the receiver up to her ear.

"Hello?" Her own voice sounded strange, unused.

The voice on the other end sounded frantic. "Annabeth Turner?"

"Yes, but my name now is Wiz—" she began to say.

"This is T. R. Reynolds, Annabeth. I . . . feel terrible, what I've done to you. I want you to listen to me very carefully. The manuscript I gave you—I want you to destroy it immediately."

"I can't do that."

Reynolds was wheezing, his breath coming in a ragged, uneven rhythm. He tried to speak once, but left off in a hacking dusty fit of coughing. "Anna . . . beth . . ."

"I can't destroy your book," Annabeth said. "It's told me everything I need to know."

"What it's told you is a lie." Reynolds shot out the words, and then lapsed into a long wheezing fight for breath.

Suddenly Annabeth felt her own throat close, as if in sympathy. The voice fighting to speak to her on the other end of the line became very faint. Her vision constricted to a whirl of images and she began to fight for breath—

Asthma attack.

Still clutching the phone with one hand, hearing T. R. Reynolds's strained voice from far away—"I was . . . made to write . . . those . . . things . . . there's nothing . . . true in . . . there. . . ."

Annabeth searched frantically with her other hand for her inhaler. It should have been in the right-hand pocket of her jeans, but it wasn't there. She dug frantically, clawing at loose change, her house keys, but it was gone.

Still hearing Reynolds's voice—"lies . . . everything lies . . . he . . ."—she dug into her other pockets, but came up empty. Her jacket was on the floor next to the desk and she reached frantically down to it, patting its pockets as her breathing became even more ragged, her throat closing—"Anna . . . beth . . . are you all . . . right?"—and suddenly she was on all fours, on the carpet, the phone dropped next to her, trying desperately to pull in air . . .

And then her hand fell on the respirator—it must have fallen out of her pocket onto the floor. She yanked it up and put it to her mouth, breathing . . . breathing. . . .

She rolled over onto her back, as precious oxygen

flowed into her lungs again and her constricted throat began to open. She closed her eyes and breathed normally, now hearing the phone—a ragged, broken chatter was coming from it. She opened her eyes and saw the receiver nearby and pulled it to her ear. She got up slowly and sat back at her desk.

"Anna . . . beth . . . can you . . . hear . . . me . . . ?"

"Yes, Mr. Reynolds, I'm all right."

"I'm . . . not . . ." His voice sounded very strained. There was a long pause filled with the same sounds she had just made and then suddenly Reynolds's voice caught and he said, very clearly, *"Oh, God."*

"Mr. Reynolds?"

"My God, my hands, my hands, *even older*—"

"Mr. Reyn—"

"Annabeth, listen to me!" His voice was rising in pitch, becoming at once more frantic and weaker. "The flesh . . . is aging before me, on my arms, my hands, *I can see my own bones*—"

There suddenly came a high, unearthly, rasping scream, which went on and on and then suddenly stopped.

Annabeth heard what sounded like a pile of something clacking, falling to the floor.

"Mr. Reynolds?" she said fearfully.

There was hissing silence on the other end of the line.

"Mr. Reynolds?"

He can't hear you, Wizard.

"Oh, no . . ."

Don't worry about him, Wizard. There are no lies in his book. Hang up the phone.

Slowly, she replaced the phone in its cradle.

"But he—"

We won't think about that. It's not important now. What's important is what you've learned. And what it's going to show you.

"Yes . . ."

Look at the manuscript again, Wizard.

Annabeth looked down at the open manuscript pages on the desk before her. She smoothed the crumpled edges, pulled at a crease that went through the middle of the left hand page. On it was the chapter title—*Eleven: the Bizarre Sightings of 1981.*

For perhaps the hundredth time in the last few days, she began to read:

> *In 1981, there occurred what remain to this day the strangest Sam sightings of them all. What made them even stranger was their seeming connection to a group of deaths that occurred on and around Halloween of that year.*

The first paragraph ended with an asterisk, which led to a note at the bottom of the page:

> *It should be noted before we proceed any further that the police department of Orangefield never considered the deaths of the Halloween season of 1981 to be anything other than coincidence, and no*

*criminal or any other kind of proceedings were ever
initiated. As police captain at the time, Owen Cas-
sidy stated: "Deaths sometimes cluster at certain
times of the year. Because three of these were homicides, with the perpetrator dead himself, I would
merely count myself lucky as far as paperwork goes.
As for the rest of them, nothing but chance is involved, or maybe the influence of a full moon—or
maybe Halloween."*

Reynolds, in the main body of the text, then got to
the heart of the matter:

*Here are the facts as they're known from records:
Between the first of October, 1981, and the last day
of the month, five deaths from unnatural causes
were recorded in Orangefield. In the previous year,
there had been no homicides, and, indeed, in the previous five years there had been three homicides in
toto recorded.*

*At the same time, during the 1981 Halloween
season, there were forty-one separate Sam sightings, up from three the previous year and ten total
for the previous five year period.*

*The first deaths, homicides, occurred on October
2nd, when a local pumpkin farmer, Bedel Mayes,
hacked his wife and infant son to death with a machete. Mayes had, the week before, reported a Sam
sighting in his own field, which was corroborated
by his field hand, Derrick Johnson. Johnson himself was killed by Mayes when he discovered the*

bodies of the first two murder victims in the barn the next day. All three victims were later found laid out in a row, rotting in the same barn; some of the farm's stock, including several pigs which had gotten loose, were reported to have eaten parts of the corpses.

Mayes then spent the rest of October going about his business and tending his pumpkins, until he killed himself on Halloween. He was found in the barn with his victims. He had attempted to decapitate himself with the same machete he had used on his family and Derrick Johnson.

A bizarre phrase (which will be discussed later, see note below) was found carved in the barn's door.

There were two other victims with ties to Sam sightings that Halloween. One, Mabel Genes, was a successful suicide who left a short note regarding not only her encounters with Sam, but the promises he had made to her. The other was an attempted suicide, a girl of eleven whose name was protected by the police and her family, but who, according to the local newspaper, the Herald, had also seen Sam and been influenced by him. She had carved a phrase into her left forearm with the end of a paper clip, which tied her to the two successful suicides (this phrase will be discussed later; again, see note below) but, after her suicide failed, she apparently had no further contact with Samhain. In fact, according to sources in the police department, the girl remembered nothing of her encounter with Sam or her attempted suicide, and the matter was kept secret.

According to one reliable source, she grew up in Orangefield and lives there to this day, unaware of her participation in the events of 1981.

This section ended in another asterisk, which led to another footnote:

The strange note of Mabel Genes, as well as the phrase from it which tied together the two suicides as well as the attempted suicide, will be discussed in detail in Chapter Fourteen: Who is Sam?

Annabeth quickly turned ahead to the place she had marked in Chapter Fourteen. She sat staring at a photograph of a middle-aged, slightly dumpy woman with a lopsided smile and kind, moist eyes. She felt she knew those eyes. The caption under the photograph read: *Mabel Genes.*

Go ahead, Wizard, finish it. Read it again. Read the secret. It's all true.

Annabeth's eyes rested on the well-read section under the photograph; she took a deep breath and read:

And now we come to the strangest item in all the modern canon of Sam sightings, the suicide note of Mabel Genes. By all accounts (and this includes newspaper articles, eyewitness reports and medical records, as well as the testimony of the present author, who knew Ms. Genes and was, in fact, a pupil in her first grade class at Orangefield Elementary at the time) Ms. Genes was gregarious, happy, happily married and well adjusted. Before Halloween of 1981 she showed absolutely no tendency toward depression or self-destruction. She was a Presbyterian and devoutly religious.

But something happened in the second week of October of 1981 to change her personality utterly. Her husband said later that she almost appeared posessed. (As a sidebar, and perhaps an irrelevant or even comical one, it should be remembered that the novel and movie The Exorcist *had been released within the previous decade.) During that week, after school, Ms. Genes made her annual visit to Froelich Farms to pick pumpkins for her classroom and home. She had been doing this for twenty-two years. While in the field, alone and at the end of the day, she reportedly had an encounter with Samhain—later she told her husband that he had risen up out of the ground like a "black whirlpool" and spoken to her.*

The incident was forgotten, except that Ms. Genes began to have strange dreams (again, as told to her husband) and exhibit increasingly bizarre behavior. This behavior—which included night walking and what appeared to be periodic trances, as well as talking when no one was there, abruptly ceased the week before Halloween, just when Mr. Genes was about to schedule her for a doctor's visit. The next week, Mrs. Genes, according to her husband and others (including the present author, who had noticed the change in his teacher and then recalled her sudden return to normalcy—she was known for her wonderful in-class Halloween party, and this party proceeded as planned, two days before the holiday) returned to normal and the matter of medical attention was dropped.

Then, early on the morning of Halloween, which was on a Friday that year, Mabel Genes was found hanging naked from the family's apple tree in the backyard.

The incident would have faded in memory if not for the bizarre suicide note that was found nailed to the tree. It was not its length (which was brief), but its enigmatic nature that have made it special in the history of Sam literature. For it opens to discussion the entire question of not only who Sam is, but what he represents. The note read, to begin with:

Sam promises life.

If, indeed, Sam is Samhain, the Celtic Lord of Death, what can this part of the note mean? Was Mabel Genes promised, by Samhain, life after death? Would Samhain have this power? If so, who gives it to him? Who does he serve?

There followed a three page discussion of religious and philosophical issues, which Annabeth had read with interest the first time and then discarded as irrelevant. For there was only one more section in the whole volume that held any interest for her. It was the phrase that Sam had drawn her attention to when she first studied the pages of *Occult Practices in Orangefield and Chicawa County, New York, Volume Two.*

Annabeth turned to it now.

Do you believe me, Wizard?

Annabeth looked up from the page, looked out the window over her desk down into her backyard, with its own tall elm tree with a sturdy rope ending in a noose hanging ready from its strongest limb.

"Yes, I believe you."

Then nothing else matters, does it?

"No."

Good, Wizard. You will do well. And you will get what you want.

"I want to see where he is. Where they all are."

It's what I promised Mabel Genes, Wizard. She lost a child which no one, not even her husband, knew about. Just like you lost your father. And you shall see it soon. Read, Wizard. Read the rest of it.

Annabeth looked down at the manuscript pages:

And now we come to the rest of Mabel Genes's suicide note, and the strangest part of all. For in it she states:

Three will show the way.

These were precisely the words that were found etched by machete into Bedel Mayes's barn door, and the same words the eleven-year-old attempted suicide had carved into her arm with the end of a paper clip.

Annabeth briefly studied her own left forearm, where crusted-over scabs covered the same words she had recently carved there with an open pair of scissors. Then she returned to the manuscript pages:

It is obvious that the "Three" refers to the three suicides.
But what will they show the way for?
Or who?

CHAPTER FORTY-THREE

It won't be long. You should be ready.

"I hope so. If I were you I'd still be worried about the girl."

The girl will be no problem. I've told you that.

"If not the girl, then interference with her."

It won't happen. And I've turned any possible interference to our advantage.

"Was this the 'insurance' you spoke of?"

Yes. I'm sure it will work.

"You said that the last time. And look what happened."

This time nothing will go wrong. You have only to be prepared.

"I hope so—*Sam*. As I said: I worry about the girl."

Even if the girl becomes a problem, there is another ready to take her place. As I said: insurance.

"Ah. . . ."

CHAPTER FORTY-FOUR

The Pumpkin Tender awoke wrapped in his Army blanket, wet, in a furrow in his favorite field. He sat up and noted that the sky, here in the new morning, was already clearing.

It would be cold and clear later.

His leg ached, and he shivered.

"Do you know what day it is, Aaron?"

He turned to see that the pumpkin with two lobes—now rotting away, the orange furrowed flesh of its face gray and soft—had grown a face again. Its mouth was downturned, its sad eyeholes roiling with worms. Its top had completely caved in.

It turned in its muddy nest with a squishing sound and looked straight at him.

"I said: Do you know what day it is, Aaron?"

The Pumpkin Tender said nothing.

The pumpkin's sagging mouth drew up slowly

into a smile, bits of rotting fruit and seeds falling from it as it did so.

"It's Halloween, Aaron."

The Pumpkin Tender still said nothing, only drew himself up tighter into his blanket.

"And that means it's time to remember, Aaron. And forget forever."

Things were so much easier this way. Now that he knew who he was, and knew what he did—and what he had to do—a kind of calm came over him.

If only he had done this a long time ago . . .

The day had turned beautiful. The morning mist had completely dissipated, leaving the day as cold and clear as any day in October could be. The sky was painfully blue, and the leaves, still clinging to trees or resting on the ground, were a gift of colors—gold, bright yellow, russet red. The air smelled of leaves and pine and Halloween itself.

He got what he needed from the little space Mr. Froelich let him use in the farm stand's storage shed, and started the long walk to the top of the mountain. His leg felt better than it had in years. On the way he saw Froelich stacking gourds for the tourists, who would come after Halloween and into Thanksgiving to fill their city homes with a little of the autumn season. He used to like Thanksgiving a lot.

Froelich stopped his work when he saw The Pumpkin Tender approach. He stretched his back and put his hands into the pockets of his overalls.

"Aaron! Was beginning to think you disappeared."

The Pumpkin Tender smiled.

"How you feeling these days, son? You did another fine job this year. We'll all look forward to next year."

The Pumpkin Tender continued to smile and limped on.

Froelich pointed at the gunny sack in Aaron's hand. "Going on a little trip?"

The Pumpkin Tender gave a short nod and kept moving.

"Well, remember, when the weather gets too cold, you come and bed down here, just like always."

Aaron waved.

The long climb went slowly, but he savored every step. He thought of Peggy and what might have been, and of the days of his childhood, which had been ideal. He had played in these hills every day after school, and hadn't had a care in the world.

Just like now.

He tried to sing out, but only a croak came from his ruined throat. It would do.

He was no longer Frankenstein. Or the Pumpkin Tender. He was just Aaron Peters, who was finally doing what had to be done.

He reached the summit in mid-afternoon. There were no full pumpkin fields to look down on now, no ring of orange fire around Orangefield. In fact, the muddy empty fruit fields that encircled the town would be cold, uninviting places for the rest of the year and well into next. But the view was still a good one, the distant town set like a jewel in the midst of wooded hills, and it was still his favorite place.

And today was Halloween.

He opened his gunny sack on the ground and laid out the contents carefully. There was a small picture of Peggy, which he had carried in his wallet when she was his girl. There was a photo of his mother and father, and another of himself the year before he went to Somalia, standing with his brother next to his Mustang—it was a good shot, and showed off the car's interior. And there was a photo of Kip Berger in his uniform, helmet tilted back on his head, smiling broadly as if nothing in the world would ever go wrong.

But of course it had, which was the whole point.

Next to the photos he lay down his Army issue .45, which was already loaded, and the note that the two-lobed pumpkin had told him to write.

Are you ready, Aaron?

He turned to see the figure in black emerge from the edge of the woods behind him and to his right. It looked like black smoke in the bright daylight, and stayed in the shadows at the edge of the tree line.

He knew he should be frightened, but for the first time since that moment in Somalia when he had pushed his friend away from the mine, he felt absolute peace and—*happiness.*

It's time, Aaron.

The black figure seemed to melt away and then re-form, but its words were right next to his ear.

Aaron nodded, and bent down to pick up the .45. The pain in his leg was gone.

Go ahead, Aaron.

He turned away from the writhing black figure

and put the .45 to his head, next to where the voice was speaking to him, and looked down at Orange-field, which was suddenly surrounded by a ring of orange, as if all the pumpkins he had ever tended had sprung back to life, just for him.

He opened his mouth in delight and made a sound of joy . . .

And pulled the trigger.

CHAPTER FORTY-FIVE

In his white cell in Killborne Hospital, Jordie heard
what sounded like a distant shot.

It must have been very loud to get through the
inches of padding on the walls. There was no window except for the tiny round one set into the door
above the food slot, and Jordie imagined there was
thick concrete behind the padding.

Weird that he could hear a gunshot.

Or anything else that wasn't in his head.

At least they'd left him his meds.

It was just about the only thing they had left him.
He couldn't remember much about the last month,
and they'd tried to stabilize him every which way
they could—with shots, electroshock, therapy—but
nothing had worked. He knew he had a silly grin on
his face, but what else could you have when basically
you were a blank? He was as blank and white as the
walls, which was just fine with him.

Maybe if they'd given him some vodka and weed his head would have straightened out.

He had said that to the shrink—one of them, at least—but if he remembered correctly, it hadn't gone over very well.

But the pills, they'd left him those.

They'd tried every day to get the combination right. But so far nothing had worked. Each day at eight in the morning and six in the evening, a little tray with a different assortment—green and yellow, yellow and white, white and blue, blue and red— was shoved through the slot, while a moony face with a bald head watched him from the little round window set in the door.

And each time he'd shrugged and taken whatever pills they'd given him.

And he stayed a blank, as blank in his head as a white sheet of paper.

Here they came again, which meant it must be eight in the morning or six at night.

He looked at the tray resting in the slot's retractable shelf and shrugged. He shuffled in his paper slippers over to the door and took the tray.

The shelf immediately retracted.

He looked for the moony face studying him, but the window was empty.

Then he heard a tinny, shrill voice behind the slot, which opened again. Now he heard the voice more clearly: "Hey nutball, it's Halloween! Happy holiday!"

He smiled and shrugged. "Whatever," he answered.

The moony face appeared in the round window, laughing at him. It was a round face for a round window, only now it wasn't bald, but had bright orange hair.

Suddenly the hair was gone and the face was bald again.

The slot pushed open again. "Like my fright wig, nutball?"

The face went away.

Jordie looked at the tray on the floor.

The pills were orange and white.

A faint connection was made: *Halloween!*

Now he recalled at least that: costumes, pumpkins, cutouts taped to windows, trick or treat, candy.

Candy. Candy corn—it had been his favorite.

He took the three pills—two orange, one white—from the tray and popped them into his mouth.

They didn't taste like candy corn, but they felt hard against the back of his throat, just like candy corn would.

Those pills will make you right, Jordie.

The voice.

Like a Pavlovian dog hearing its signal, Jordie immediately began to look for his list. But there were no pockets in the orange jumpsuit. He dropped to all fours and began to search the cell, looking behind the toilet, the bolted-in white sink, under the one-piece steel cot with a single sheet covering the foam mattress and the flimsy pillow. He pulled the pillow out of its pillowcase, turning it inside out, studying it closely.

It had to be in there, it was the only place the list could be.

No need for lists anymore, Jordie. Don't worry about it.

There it was again, the voice. He hadn't heard it since they'd packed him off to this place after that mess at the police hearing—*Schizophrenic delusions, paranoia, violence brought on by medication imbalance, the abuse of narcotics and alcohol.*

He remembered that hearing well enough.

Do you remember what you did, Jordie?

"Not much."

Would you like to?

"I don't think so."

What do you remember?

He sat down cross-legged on the floor and tossed the pillowcase aside. "I remember I stopped taking my meds. Just like you told me."

That's right. And what did you do after that?

"I did some bad stuff. That's what they tell me. But I remember a rockin' dj gig in there. Pumpkin Days. Best show I ever put on." He smiled, letting the beat of his music come into his head.

What about the bad stuff you did, Jordie? Do you recall any of it?

Still hearing a heavy techno *thump-thump* inside his head, he said, "No way. Don't remember any of it. But I bet my mom'll give it to me good, if I ever get out of this place."

Soon you're going to remember all of it. Every second of it. The pills you took are the ones you need to stabilize you, Jordie. You'll be as normal as before you met me. I've been . . . shall we say, fiddling with your medications for a couple of days. The various combinations made you do some very interesting things.

"Cool," Jordie said, working his hands like they held drum sticks. "Did I do anything funny? I used to do funny things when I was a kid. Once I jumped off the roof of Josh's garage, on a dare. And not at the bottom of the roof, but at the top, where it came to a point. Broke my friggin' ankle. Rode my bike into a wall once, too. That's when they found out I needed the meds."

There's not much funny about what you've done lately, Jordie.

"Huh." A sudden clear image swirled into his head, then out again. He stopped his drumming motions. Him, pushing a knife into Josh's belly, in his kitchen. "Weird."

The music started up again in his head, and again it stopped when another image swirled in, his aunt begging for her life in front of the fireplace in their house, on her knees in front of him covered in blood, screaming for him not to . . .

"Whoa." The music was gone, replaced by nightmares. He went into a fetal position on the cement floor and closed his eyes, willing the images to go away. But they were getting more and more real—him holding a blade up, licking blood from it, a sawing sound as he worked on the body in the chair, the heads lined up on the kitchen counter . . .

"Make it stop! Make it stop!" he gasped, pulling at his own head.

But the voice was silent.

The images connected into scenes now, and he

saw everything as it became more and more clear: what he had done to his friend Josh, what he had done to his aunt, *what he had done to his mother. . . .*

A long hiss of pain escaped him, but still the images became even more distinct: the bodies in the cellar, him propping them up, covering them in lime, putting them into poses, his roasting and eating his aunt's hand—

There's only one way to make it all go away, Jordie.

They were so real now, so much a part of what he'd done, so much of what he was—

They'll discover that the meds have balanced you, Jordie. The memories will never go away again.

He opened his eyes and said in sobbing awe, "I did these things?"

Oh, yes, Jordie, you did them all. And you'll never forget. Unless you do what I say. . . .

He quickly followed the voice's instructions. First he left a message, gouging his wrist with his teeth until there was enough blood flowing to write on the wall. Then he fashioned what he needed from strips of the single sheet on the bed. One end of the makeshift rope he secured around the faucet of the sink, and then he sat on the floor and tied the other end around his neck.

Quickly, Jordie, before they find you and make you remember forever.

He had a momentary lapse of nerve and the remembrance of what he'd done came rushing back into his head, all of it at once, like a large-screen movie, the silence in the house, the smell and taste of blood, the bits of flesh under his fingernails—

Now, Jordie. Just fall over.

He did as he was told.

Good.

And then a miraculous thing happened. The horror movie in his head was turned off. He was on the top of Josh's roof again, at the apex, making windmill motions in the air with his arms and shouting, "Will you laugh? Will you laugh?"

The day was bright and sunny, and he felt warm air rush by his face as he jumped, shouting gleefully, hearing the whoops of disbelief and wonder from his friends, and then he hit the ground—

CHAPTER FORTY-SIX

The doorbell rang.

As Kathy Marks hurried to answer, it rang again, twice, insistent, with a murmur of voices behind it.

"Coming!" she called out.

She opened the door to another gaggle of costumed children. This group was composed of three pirates, with appropriate black buccaneer hats bearing skull and crossbones, blood-red scarves knotted around their necks and cutlasses. One of them had a plastic knife clenched in his teeth.

"Aaargh! Trick or treat!" the other two shouted.

Kathy smiled and dipped into her black plastic cauldron filled with candy. The pirates greedily watched the booty go into their bags.

"Thank you!" they cried, sounding very much like children as they bounded off her porch, making way for a mixed group of space aliens and witches behind them.

There was a lull after this bunch, and Kathy folded her arms against the chill and leaned against the open door. The night was perfect for Halloween—cold and crisp, with a nearly full moon rising over the houses across the street. There were pumpkins everywhere, carved and lit, faces alive, faint breeze stirring their fires within. Every porch light was on, and, because this was Orangefield, many houses sported more than the usual window decorations of skeletons, broomstick-borne witches and black cats. Most were lit with orange bulbs across their gutters, and two were involved in their annual battle to outdo one another, with full-size monsters—Dracula on one lawn, a mummy on his neighbor's—guarding their homes. The street was alive with marching costumed children, mostly in bunches, their adult chaperones safely warm in vehicles at the curb; there was a veritable caravan of cars, minivans and SUVs crawling up one side of the street and down the next. Distant cries of "Trick or treat!" wafted through the air like falling autumn leaves.

A perfect Halloween.

But Kathy still couldn't get Annabeth Turner off her mind.

Shivering, she closed the door and walked through her neatly furnished living room into her small, tidy kitchen, punching the girl's number again on her wall phone and waiting while it rang. She was about to hang up after ten rings when a click on the other end announced that someone had picked it up.

"Hello?" Kathy said hopefully into the receiver.

"Wha..? Whoosit?"

It was Annabeth's mother, obviously drunk. "Mrs. Turner, this is Kathy Marks—"

"Tol' you stay 'way! No damn social services—"

Fearing the woman would hang up, she interrupted her. "Mrs. Turner, is Annabeth home?"

"Who? Don' know. Mus' be a dream . . ." As if coming to her senses, she added, "Tol' you no social—"

Kathy hung up the phone.

At that moment she decided she had to make sure the girl was all right.

She was suddenly sure that protecting Annabeth Turner was what she had been waiting for all these years.

She stood looking at the phone for a moment, something dancing at the edges of her mind, and absently rubbed at her left forearm.

Faintly impressed there, mostly hidden by years of scarring, were the words, which had been carved with an opened paper clip many years ago, an act which she didn't remember:

Three will show the way

She threw on a coat and filled the candy cauldron to the brim with all the candy she had bought. Leaving now, at the height of trick-or-treating, was sacrilegious, and she could expect her house to be at least egged, if not shaving-creamed or worse. But she taped a hastily written note to the front of the cauldron and set it up on a planter stand on the porch after locking the front door. The note read: *Take Just One, Please!*

She had no doubt the candy would be gone, and quickly, when that note was ignored, but it was the best she could do.

She had some trouble getting out of her driveway—a minivan was blocking it, and the driver was nowhere to be seen.

But then she appeared, dragging a wailing bat-costumed boy of about five after her, shouting, "I told you, eight o'clock! You have enough candy!"

She pushed him, still wailing, into the van and drove off.

The night was alive. Things seemed a little more frantic this year, a little more on edge, a little more electric than usual. Maybe it was the cold coming on the heels of the earlier October warmth. There was a meanness in the air that normally wasn't present. Kathy felt a prickling in her skin, as if the sky was alive with black autumn, with Halloween itself.

There were lights from pumpkins, porches and decorations everywhere along the few blocks she had to navigate to the main road. A group of teens, who seemed to be talking on a street corner, suddenly turned when she stopped at the stop sign and, cackling, lobbed eggs at her car. Two eggs hit the passenger side window and stayed there, like yellow eyes. She swerved, cursing herself for doing so— they were only *eggs,* for heavens sake—but the look on their faces, pinched, almost malevolent, made her step on the gas and speed away. She heard them hoot after her, and watched them in the rearview mirror physically attack the car behind her as it stopped, smearing eggs over the windshield and climbing up onto its roof.

She kept a little above the speed limit after that, until she entered the Turner's neighborhood.

Things were pretty much the same here as on her own street, except for the Turner house, which was dark. Already there were long lines of shaving cream across the front windows and siding, and the mailbox was covered with broken eggs. As Kathy got out of the car she saw a little girl, dressed as a princess with tiara and gold slippers, standing in the street, crying. At her feet was a dropped sack, spilling candy.

Kathy took a step toward the girl and as if out of nowhere a woman appeared, shouting, "Get away from her!"

Kathy froze as the woman grabbed the girl with one hand, scooped up the spilled bag with the other, and hustled both off down the street, leaving a small scattered pile of candy bars and tiny candy boxes behind.

Somewhere a dog howled, long and mournful.

The moon, high in the east now, yellow as squash, was occluded by scudding clouds.

Kathy walked to the Turner's front door, stepping over a broken pumpkin and an abandoned bicycle wheel.

A convertible full of teenagers roared by, shouting abuse. A line of eggs flew to Kathy's right, peppering the already vandalized house.

The front door stood wide open.

Kathy put her head into the darkened entry and said, "Hello?"

A cat, fat and dark orange, hissed and ran out past her into the night.

From somewhere in the back of the house, beyond the stairway to the second floor, came a mournful sound, a miniature of the dog's howl she had heard.

She stepped into the house, nudging aside a lopsided pile of newspapers that blocked the hallway with her foot. The pile collapsed, papers spilling like playing cards.

The pained sound came again.

"*Ohhhh.*"

"Mrs. Turner, it's Kathy Marks. I'm in your house."

"*Ohhhhhh.*"

Kathy slowly walked down the hallway, passing the living room, which was filled with deep shadows—furniture at odd angles, boxes that looked as if they had never been unpacked.

The sound came again from the kitchen.

Kathy stepped into the dimly lit room. There was a low-wattage bulb under the stove hood, which was the only steady illumination. A round ceiling fluorescent bulb flashed once, stayed off. Everything looked orange. There was an open, unlit refrigerator, a door to the backyard blocked by an open garbage can beside it, the smell of bad eggs and sour milk, a small rectangular kitchen table with a window over it covered with filthy dishes.

On a chair pulled up to the table at an angle facing the room was the slumped figure of Mrs. Turner.

"Ohhhhh . . ."

Mrs. Turner tried to raise her head, but only managed to lift it high enough to moan again. Her face was bleary with drink. She lifted her right hand slightly, trying to reach the nearly empty gin bottle, which teetered on the edge of the table. There was vomit in a pool on the table and on her left arm, on which she lay her head.

"Ohhhh, dreaming . . ."

Her right hand fell against the bottle, knocking it off the table. It fell but didn't break, sloshing some of the remaining clear liquid on the dirty floor.

Mr. Turner sent up a louder wail.

Kathy Marks approached. "Mrs. Turner, your daughter . . ."

"Dreaming!" Mrs. Turner screeched, throwing herself back on the chair and pointing with a wavering right hand out the window behind her. She fell partially forward, now spying the clear bottle on the ground, and pushed her chair violently back, dropping to the floor and scrambling after the remains of the gin.

Out through the window Kathy saw movement in the moonlight: a figure and something under a tree . . .

The librarian leaned forward, around the moaning figure of Annabeth's mother, and peered out the window.

"My God!"

Annabeth Turner was trying to kick aside a chair

that supported her. A rope suspended her by the neck from a sturdy branch of the tree. As the librarian watched, the chair fell aside, letting the girl swing free, arms at her sides.

"Annabeth!" Kathy Marks screamed, moving frantically to her right. She pushed aside the garbage can blocking the back door, knocking it over, spilling fruit peels and used slices of lime. She yanked the door open.

There were three wooden steps down to ground level. The top slat broke, sending her foot through and catching painfully at the ankle. She pulled it out, ignoring the pain.

She ran for the girl.

The moon overhead was completely covered by clouds at that moment. The night became darker and colder.

Far off she heard the beginning of a roar, and the ground began to tremble.

Dogs howled as if in unison, and every light in Orangefield, as if on cue, went out.

The night was filled with a hush, followed by an unearthly, keening cry. Overhead the sky became impossibly dark, and a darker shape, boiling out like black ink, began to fill the heavens where stars and the moon had been.

The girl became still.

"Annabeth! No!"

Kathy Marks grabbed Annabeth by her middle and held her up. She was a dead, cold weight. The librarian tried to upright the fallen chair with her foot. Moaning with frustration, she let the girl down and quickly reached down and set the chair on its legs, then stood on it and took Annabeth in her arms again, lifting her against her own body while she worked at the noose, loosening it, then tearing it away from Annabeth's neck.

She lowered the girl to the ground.

"Annabeth!"

The girl lay cold and still, and the librarian took her by the shoulders and shook her.

"Annabeth, please!"

The girl gave a choking gasp and looked straight up at the librarian.

"Nothing!" she cried. "I saw nothing but an airless place, a desert! He lied!"

Around them, the keening sound retreated, deeper darkness retreated, the lights in the houses around them blinked back on.

The night was filled with a sudden deathly silence. The moon slid from behind its clouds.

Not her. You, Kathy. Finally, time to remember.

Kathy Marks gasped, looked around her frantically.

That voice. Like the voice at the library—like a voice she suddenly remembered from so long ago . . .

Time to finish it, this time, Kathy. Remember . . .

Memories, which had been locked safely away since she was eleven, began to flood back into her, a jumble of unrelated images, and she gasped again—

Don't you remember, Kathy? Remember it all now. . . .

It all came screaming back at her, suddenly sharp and clear, as if the door to a locked room had been kicked open.

A cold Halloween, colder than she ever remembered . . .

She ate her cold cereal at the breakfast table with her aunt and uncle, just like always. Uncle Edward was in a sour mood this morning, some trouble at the bank—but, as always when he left, after carefully folding his newspaper and leaving it next to his empty egg cup and plate of toast, his empty orange juice glass and coffee cup, he rose and pecked his wife on the cheek and kissed Kathy on the top of her head. Today he pushed something into Kathy's hand and whispered, "For Halloween. Have fun." As he was leaving, closing the front door behind him she looked down to see two crisp dollar bills, folded in half, in her hand.

Aunt Jane's hand quickly covered her own and pried the money loose. "I'll take those," she said primly, unfolding and studying the money, then making a snorting sound before putting it in the cookie jar, a fat green bear, on the shelf on the wall over the table. She gave Kathy a cold look. "Finish your cereal and get off to school. You'll understand when you're older." Then she added, "Or maybe you won't." She was staring toward the closed front door as the sound of her husband's car faded down the street. After a moment she spoke again, in a soft voice, still facing the front door. "Just because you're his kin don't make you mine. When your ma and pa died I told Edward not to take you in. I told him five times. But he didn't listen. He said your pa was his brother, and that made him beholden." Annabeth

saw that her hands were trembling, and a single tear
tracked her hard, pinched face. "I told him," she
said, a dry, bitter sob.

School was school. At lunchtime she talked with her
friend Mary for a while, then went off by herself, behind the big elm, to talk to Sammy.

"How are you today?" Sammy asked, in a particularly jolly voice.

"Fine. How are you?"

"You know I'm fine, because it's *Halloween!*"

Sammy gave a laugh, and Kathy couldn't help
smiling.

"How are things at home, Kathy? Mr. Marks still
being bad at night, after the lights go out?"

Kathy said nothing and her face darkened.

"Oh, don't be cross! You know we've talked all
about it. You know you can tell me anything."

"Yes . . . ," Kathy said in a whisper; she was thinking about the two crisp dollars in her hand that
morning.

"Did you put that fun mark on your arm, the way
I asked?"

"No," Kathy said, looking at the ground.

"Why not?" Kathy knew he would be angry, but
he wasn't as angry as she'd feared. There was still
happiness in his voice. Still staring at the ground,
she drew the large paper clip from her pocket.

"And there it is!" Sammy laughed. "Why don't we
do it now—we've got time!"

For perhaps the fifth time, Kathy carefully unbent
the outer section of the clip, making it straight. She

315

could tell that it was weakening, and if she bent it closed again in would break. She poked idly at the point with her finger.

"Aw, don't worry, it won't hurt! I won't let it!"

Again he laughed.

Holding the paper clip in her right hand, she turned over her left forearm and pressed the tip into the flesh. She pushed it in harder, seeing a drop of red blood rise from the skin.

"Now just make the words!" Sammy encouraged.

"Hey, Kathy—"

Her friend Mary was suddenly standing there, eyes wide. She stared at Kathy's arm, at the paper clip.

"What are you doing?" Mary asked.

"Nothing." Kathy lowered the paper clip, hiding it in her right palm.

"Who were you talking to?"

"Nobody," Kathy answered.

Mary shook her head. "They were right about you. I was going to invite you to trick or treat with me later, but you're *whacko*."

Mary turned and ran off.

"Hmmm?" Sammy asked, after a moment.

Kathy drew the paper clip out again, and began to carve words into the flesh of her arm as Sammy encouraged her and laughed.

Just as Sammy had predicted, they sent her home after the nurse examined what she had done to her arm. Mrs. Marks and a beating were waiting, and then there would be no trick-or-treating.

And then Mr. Marks would come home from the bank, and night would come. . . .

"But we don't care about any of that, do we?" Sammy said. "Because today you're going to see your ma and pa, right?"

"Yes . . ."

Walking down Main Street from the school toward home, Kathy noted a few strange things: an ambulance screeching through traffic toward the hospital, and then another from the opposite direction, and then, two blocks along, a crowd gathered around the front of the bank, and police cars.

"Let's go into the park!" Sammy said suddenly. It was the first time she had ever heard him sound like a grown-up—almost in a hurry.

She crossed the street and entered Rainier Park. The trees near the main road were covered with toilet paper. Farther on, the park was almost empty. She passed a few mothers with babies in strollers, all of them bundled up against the cold. Some of the babies wore Halloween costumes, cat whiskers, pink angel's wings. A touch football game was just breaking up; the football, tossed errantly, came to a rolling stop at her feet and she stood looking down at it until an older boy came and scooped it up. He paused to look into Kathy's face, and at her scabbed arm.

"Man, you're *weird*," he said and ran off, scooping up the ball.

Keep walking, Sammy said, and suddenly his voice was a bit more urgent. He had begun to talk inside her head. *You know the spot.*

Kathy was cutting diagonally across the park, toward its farthest borders. There was a grove of trees here. It was the site of picnics in the summer, with its permanently mounted barbecue grills, but once the weather chilled it became almost empty. Kathy had seen no one here the last time she had visited, the day before. There was no one now.

"Ah!" Sammy said. His voice was natural and jolly again. He seemed to be walking along beside her, though she couldn't see him.

And then she *could* see him, his black cape that swirled in and out of focus, like fog, his laughing face hidden, a hint of chalk white . . .

"It's still here, Kathy! Just like we left it!"

She stopped before a huge oak, one branch reaching out over its own fallen leaves like a long thick arm. From it hung a perfect hangman's noose. Below it was a three-legged stool Kathy had stolen from Uncle Edward's basement bar.

"What do you say, Kathy?" Sammy laughed, but then he became very urgent indeed.

Do it.

Kathy heard a faraway noise, a group of voices growing louder, but then Sammy was filling her head with his voice:

Do it now, Kathy. Climb onto the stool. You'll see your ma and pa. Put the rope around your neck. Just like I promised. Tighten the noose. Kick the stool away.

Away—

Kick it—

Away!

And then she was floating in the air, her ears filled with a roaring sound, Sammy's laughing voice, other sounds like voices carrying across a crashing surf. She felt the faint cold breeze of her own swinging body, then something very indistinct opened in front of her and the voices all went very far away, pulled down a long tunnel away from her like chattering little mice and before her was a flat and desolate place with strange shapes . . .

"Ms. Marks!"

She was in two places at once—then and now. She was yanked back and was there, in 1981, feeling her body hoisted up and opening her eyes and choking, gagging, unable to breathe, the boy with the football gawking at her from below, a policeman, and the other men who were lifting her while another ripped the noose from her neck . . .

And now, in the present, she opened her eyes and saw that she had climbed up onto Annabeth's chair, put Annabeth's rope around her neck, and kicked the chair away—

Now, Kathy. Finish it. Not like when you were eleven, not like the second time after your boyfriend Corrie Phaeder left you. Go there. Third time's the charm. See your ma and pa.

Annabeth was standing in front of her, screaming. Then she turned and ran toward the house. There was a great commotion and noise, and then the girl reappeared, running toward the tree, a long knife in her hand.

319

"Cut you down . . . ," the librarian heard Anna-beth say.

Kathy began to struggle, trying to reach up and release the pressure on her neck.

Finish it or I'll take the girl.

Annabeth stopped halfway to the tree and began to fight for breath. She collapsed, the knife falling from her grip, and began to writhe on the ground. The caped figure materialized over her like a swirling black cloud. For a brief moment it turned its cowl toward Kathy and she saw a horrid paste-white face within, black holes for eyes and a thin red-lipped mouth in the shape of a perfect O, full of emptiness.

She dies unless you finish it.

The girl was fighting to draw something from her pocket and then found it, an inhaler. It rolled from her grasping fingers onto the grass.

Do it now.

Kathy let go and closed her eyes.

"All right," she sighed.

And then she began to lose consciousness, felt the weight on her neck squeezing, Sammy's own fingers squeezing the air from her—

"Ha ha!" Sammy laughed happily. "Time to fin-ish it!"

She felt the ground begin to tremble again, heard the hush followed by a high keen, darkness enclos-ing the earth, the stars and moon blotted out, that flat and airless and empty place below her—

"Time to see ma and pa!" Sammy yelled.

As when she was eleven, the dry and airless desert opened in front of her, and what had been only bright clouds began to form into something else, shapes, moving shapes . . .

And now for the briefest moment she thought she saw—

"Ha ha ha—"

A curtain dropped down. She fell. Air came back into her lungs and Sammy's voice was gone, shut off in mid-laugh.

Slowly, the night came back to her. She heard the sound of a dog barking, the laughter of children, a far-off shout of "Trick or treat!" She felt the cold of the autumn night breeze on her face, and the wetness of dewey grass on her fingers.

She felt sweet cold air in her lungs.

Kathy slowly opened her eyes.

Annabeth Turner knelt on the grass beside her. The inhaler was pressed tightly to her mouth. She drew a long ragged breath and then lowered the inhaler.

"You—" Kathy began.

"I wouldn't let him take you," she said.

The librarian raised herself on her elbows. She saw the knife and the cut noose beside her on the grass. She looked at Annabeth, who was suddenly crying.

"He promised to show me—"

"I . . . saw . . . ," Kathy Marks began. "I . . . saw . . . *something*. . . ."

The young girl fell into her arms, crying, and Kathy held her for a long time.

* * *

Around them, Halloween went on. The moon came out from hiding, became sharp and white and round with a smirking face. On porches, candled pumpkins flickered bright, and, up and down streets, children dressed as monsters of a thousand kinds pounded on doors demanding candy, and filled handled bags and pillow cases to the brim with goodies. Trees rattled their bone branches and made the wind moan through their wooden instruments. Black cats tiptoed under circling, flapping bats.

And then a curious thing happened. There came curfew, and then midnight. The pumpkins lost their fiery faces, the monsters scattered, and the porch lights went dark and the window cutouts were hard to see. The winking Halloween lights went off, and the papier-mâché spiders went to sleep in their vast rope webs.

The world went quiet.

Tomorrow it would all be gone, all of it.

Halloween was over.

CHAPTER FORTY-SEVEN

"You've failed."

That's true. What are you going to do, kill me?

"You're usually not one for levity. You must know how disappointed I am."

We've tried this twice now, and it hasn't worked. Perhaps it's time to try other things.

"I agree. We have few enough opportunities. Though, as you realize, it will be more difficult."

As I said, these . . . creatures are fascinating in many ways. A mixture of weakness and tenacity and, sometimes, surprising strength. The girl and the woman, and the detective, Grant . . .

"You sound as if you almost developed feeling for them. They were the reason you failed."

They were too strong, and, ultimately, too resilient.

"Perhaps we should avoid females in the future, and police detectives."

Perhaps. But there's a toughness in many of them, regardless of gender.

"Would you like to return to the time of burning wicker men, stuffed with goat innards and human criminals? Or perhaps to an earlier time still, when they crawled on all fours through their own fetid muck—"

Your own levity is noted, Dark One.

"They have known both of us by many names since the beginning of this wretched place. They will know me again."

I shall succeed for you yet.

"And then I will rid this world of every speck of life."

Yes. I'm glad I let the girl and woman possess the merest hint . . .

"Hint of what?"

Never mind. My own realm. Don't be alarmed.

"For someone who's failed me, you show a remarkably cavalier attitude. It seems to me we have much work to do."

Yes. There's always next Halloween. . . .

GRAHAM MASTERTON

NIGHT WARS

They are five ordinary people, forced to do battle on the most terrifying field imaginable—the landscape of nightmares. They are the Night Warriors and only they can defeat the evil that has invaded our world through our dreams.

Two of the cruelest and most horrific apparitions ever seen are attempting to destroy our world by entering the dreams of expectant mothers. They bring with them armies of nightmare creatures, horrible beings that could only spring from someone's worst fear. It is against these demons, in an unreal world of terror, that the five Night Warriors must prepare to fight the...

NIGHT WARS

SARAH PINBOROUGH

BREEDING GROUND

Life was good for Matt and Chloe. They were in love and looking forward to their new baby. But what Chloe gives birth to isn't a baby. It isn't even human. It's an entirely new species that uses humans only for food—and as hosts for their young.

As Matt soon learns, though, he is not alone in his terror. Women all over town have begun to give birth to these hideous creatures, spidery nightmares that live to kill—and feed. As the infestation spreads and the countryside is reduced to a series of web-shrouded ghost towns, will the survivors find a way to fight back? Or is it only a matter of time before all of mankind is reduced to a…BREEDING GROUND

JACK KETCHUM

OFF SEASON

September. A beautiful New York editor retreats to a lonely cabin on a hill in the quiet Maine beach town of Dead River—off season—awaiting her sister and friends. Nearby, a savage human family with a taste for flesh lurks in the darkening woods, watching, waiting for the moon to rise and night to fall....

And before too many hours pass, five civilized, sophisticated people and one tired old country sheriff will learn just how primitive we all are beneath the surface...and that there are no limits at all to the will to survive.